BEWARE!!
DO NOT READ THIS
BOOK FROM
BEGINNING TO END!

Welcome to Camp Running Leaf!

It's the sports camp of your dreams! But this place is *weird*. The coaches are slave drivers. The campers act like little robots. And the food... well, let's just say it's nothing to write home about.

The activities sound cool, though! You can camp overnight and look for bones in Zombie Cave. Coach says you could win a medal — or become one of the walking dead. Aww, he was just kidding about the dead part. *Wasn't he?*

Or you can compete in the "Selection." It's an awesome obstacle course, with stuff like water jumps. Only, hold on. Why is that water *squirming*?

You're in control of this scary adventure. You decide what will happen. And how terrifying the scares will be.

Start on PAGE 1. Follow the instructions at the bottom of each page. You make the choices. Make the right choices, and you'll have the summer of your dreams. Make the wrong choice... and it's CAMPER BEWARE!

So take a deep breath. Cross your fingers. And turn to PAGE 1 to *GIVE YOURSELF GOOSE-BUMPS!*

READER BEWARE —
YOU CHOOSE THE SCARE!

**Look for more
GIVE YOURSELF GOOSEBUMPS adventures
from R.L. STINE**

"All right!" you say to yourself.

Ten minutes ago, it looked as if you were facing another boring day at home. All the kids in your neighborhood are away at summer camp. All but you. Your parents decided to take you on a family vacation instead. To your grandparents' farm.

Boring!

But your mom and dad just got an urgent call to join a dig for dinosaur bones in Mongolia. They're leaving in the morning.

"We'll be away for a month," your mom says. "Sorry, sweetie, but we'll have to send you to Camp Pendleton after all."

"I guess I'll live," you reply, hiding your grin.

Yes!

Pendleton is a sports camp. You love sports! You've wanted to go to Camp Pendleton ever since your uncle Ed told you about it. It's got the latest equipment and the best coaches.

You quickly call Uncle Ed with the good news. He promises to take care of all the arrangements. He'll even drive you there!

The next morning, Uncle Ed arrives. Your parents are rushing around, getting ready to leave. They kiss you good-bye and remind you to be careful.

"Don't worry about me," you reply. "What could go wrong?"

Nothing, right? Hah! Turn to PAGE 2.

2

"I'm psyched!" you announce as you slide into Uncle Ed's station wagon.

"You're going to have a great time!" Uncle Ed declares.

Your uncle usually doesn't talk much about himself. You aren't even sure what he does for a living. But you do know he likes sports. That's what you talk about on the way to Camp Pendleton.

Only it's taking forever to get there. It's out in the boondocks. All the roads here look the same.

You stop for a snack. Uncle Ed makes a quick phone call. When he starts the car again, he pulls out onto the road — going in the wrong direction!

"Uncle Ed," you say, "I think you're going the wrong way."

"Nah," Uncle Ed says. "I've got a great sense of direction."

You spot an old man in front of a lone house in the woods.

"Pull over, Uncle Ed," you urge. "Let's ask."

"Sports camp?" The old man frowns. "There's a camp about a mile away." He gives Uncle Ed instructions to get there. "If you pass the gas station, you'll know you've gone too far."

"See, I told you I knew where I was going," Uncle Ed says.

Turn to PAGE 3.

A minute later, Uncle Ed turns down a dirt road. He pulls up to a military-looking gatehouse. A big sign says WELCOME TO CAMP RUNNING LEAF.

Huh?

"Where's Camp Pendleton?" you cry.

Uncle Ed only shrugs. He doesn't seem very upset.

A beefy guy with a crew cut, a white shirt, and a whistle around his neck approaches your car.

"I'm Coach Rex," he says. "Are you a new camper?"

"No, I'm looking for Camp Pendleton," you answer.

Coach Rex clears his throat. "Uh — this *was* Camp Pendleton. A new owner just took over and changed the name to Running Leaf."

So everything is okay. Right?

You say good-bye to Uncle Ed. He shakes hands with Coach Rex. "Work this youngster hard," he orders.

"Oh, I'm a slave driver," Coach Rex answers with a chuckle.

Coach Rex and Uncle Ed laugh like two old friends.

Go on to PAGE 4.

Coach Rex leads you to a cabin. He points out an empty bunk, and you drop your stuff on it.

"Think you're a hotshot athlete?" he shouts.

Surprised, you stutter, "No, um, I-I just like sports."

Coach Rex barks, "We don't put up with wimps here." He gives you the once-over. "You don't look very strong."

You thought you were in pretty decent shape. But . . .

"Let's arm wrestle," Coach Rex demands.

What's his problem? He seemed so friendly a minute ago.

You sit at opposite sides of a table. Coach Rex pins your arm in an instant. He looks disappointed. "Kid, you don't have what it takes," he announces. "But you will . . . and soon."

It sounds more like a threat than a promise.

Suddenly, Coach Rex brightens. "The first thing for you to do is to choose one of two events to take part in."

One event is an overnight hike and fossil-hunt in the woods around the camp. You love camping out. Sounds cool!

The other event is called the "Selection." It's a series of athletic events. The winner gets a special prize.

So which are you going to choose?

If you pick the hike, turn to PAGE 78.
If you pick the Selection, turn to PAGE 125.

Forget Brad! You streak down the track.

A glance over your shoulder shows Brad slowly crawling away from the snakes. V-e-r-y slowly. By the time he gets to his feet, you've crossed the finish line.

Rex grabs your arm and raises it in the air. "The winner!"

You can't believe it. You've won! You get the special prize. You get the bike. But most of all, you'll get to escape!

As you're led to the victory stand, the coaches cheer. You blink in the bright sunlight and follow Coach Rex.

"Congratulations!" he bellows. "You have proved yourself the best camper of them all. You have been Selected!"

You beam. But your smile fades as Coach Rex goes on.

"As the best human specimen, you won't work the mines, like the other, inferior campers. The blue eggs have made them strong enough to carry klatu crystals. The eggs have also made them obedient, so they'll be fine slaves. You, on the other hand, will serve the Overmaster of Xentron. With this honor comes much pain, and eventually a gruesome death."

Say what?

Did you hear Coach Rex correctly?

Go on to PAGE 29.

6

Several zombies form a line in front of you. The tall one at the front stands shakily on one leg. It holds its other leg in its hands. "UURRRRGH!" it moans, thrusting the leg at you.

"It wants you to sew its leg back on," Kim whispers.

"UURRGH!" a third zombie moans. This zombie is carrying one hand and one foot. It holds them out to you.

Some zombies are worse off than others. The most newly dead are in good shape. But the old ones are really falling apart. And they want *you* to put them back together!

You hand Kim a needle and thread. "Help me!" you order.

For the next hour, the two of you sew rotting arms, legs, hands, and feet back onto their owners. The stench is incredible. Your hands are covered with worms and bits of oozing flesh.

"I can't take this anymore!" Kim moans.

"Shut up and sew!" you command.

Finally, you're done. Every zombie who needed repairs has gotten them. You stand back and admire your work.

Then the worst thing in the world happens.

Just what is *the worst thing in the world? If you really want to know, you can find out on PAGE 73.*

Even Brad seems shaken by Coach Rex's words. He mutters to you, "Did you eat the eggs?"

"No," you answer.

"I hate eggs," Brad says. "So I gave mine to my friends. Then they all started acting weird — like they couldn't think for themselves."

It's the same thing you noticed. You can't believe what you're thinking, but . . .

"Could the eggs be controlling their minds?" you whisper.

"Oh, get real," Brad scoffs. But his voice shakes a little.

You shrug. "All I know is, I want to get out of here — and fast. This camp is scary."

"Listen up!" Coach Rex barks. You and Brad jump.

"The next event is the high bar," the coach goes on. "After that, the javelin. Then the two athletes with the highest point totals will go on to the final event."

The gymnastics coach points at you. "Get ready for your routine," he orders.

You bend down and dust your hands with rosin. But when you straighten up and glance at the bar, you can't believe your eyes.

Flames are shooting up from the ground under the high bar!

Go on to PAGE 62.

A dozen coaches stand in a circle. They're holding javelins. And they're pointing them at the contestants!

"What are these guys doing at the javelin throw?" you ask.

"Javelin throw?" Coach Rex lets out a harsh laugh. "This is the javelin *catch*!"

Uh-oh!

The sharp javelins come raining down. Dozens of gleaming metal points whiz toward you.

One of them is zooming straight for your head!

With a quick move, you barely sidestep the javelin. Its sharp point thunks into the ground. Inches from your foot.

"If you don't catch one," Coach Rex bellows, "you lose!"

More of the deadly spears shoot down. You dance back and forth, ducking them.

You can do this, you tell yourself. You've seen superheroes do it in the movies. Piece of cake, right?

Turn to PAGE 70.

You'd rather risk the rapids than keep walking — especially since it's getting so late. Anyway, you think, you're not stealing the boat — you're simply borrowing it.

You and Kim climb in. The current carries you downstream so swiftly, you don't even bother to row.

"We should reach Zombie Cave in a few minutes!" you exclaim.

"All this rocking is making me sick!" Kim whines. She does look a little green. "This was a dumb idea."

She could be right, you think, worried. The current is getting faster. And now you're starting to see big rocks in the river. The water foams white up ahead.

"Hold on!" you shout to Kim.

CRACK! A big rock knocks Kim's oar out of her hand.

CRACK! Your oar breaks in two.

The roar of the river grows louder. Off to your left, you spot a small stream. But that's not where the noise comes from. It comes from that tall spray of white water rising into the air dead ahead. . . .

A waterfall!

Better think fast!

Jump overboard on PAGE 76.
Try to steer toward the small stream on PAGE 60.

Your mouth snaps shut.

"What's with the blue eggs?" you demand.

Just then a voice comes over the loudspeaker. It's Coach Rex. "Eat up, campers! The Selection is coming, and your eggs are packed with the protein you need."

You ask Pat, "Are you going to eat your eggs?"

He shakes his head. "No way." He picks up a piece of toast and nibbles on it.

You eye your eggs. You don't normally eat blue food — except blue M&M's, of course. Who *doesn't* eat blue M&Ms?

But you don't want to act different from everyone else. Especially on your first day.

Blue eggs. Should you eat them? Or get rid of them?

Or — use them to start a food fight?

If you eat the eggs, turn to PAGE 64.

If you hide them in your napkin, turn to PAGE 94.

If you throw them at the kid across the table from you, turn to PAGE 39.

You do a fast U-turn and return to shore.

"Coach Karla! Help!" you cry. "One of the kids went down!"

Karla comes to the edge of the water. "We've got it all under control!" she snaps. "Don't worry about the other competitors! Just worry about winning the race. Now get moving!"

Confused, you start back through the soupy water. If they've got it under control, where are the rescue boats?

Then you start thinking:

What if something *pulled* that kid under the water?

Something alive. Something hungry.

Like an alligator.

Know what? That's exactly what happened.

The thing is, one kid isn't nearly enough for a hungry alligator. A hungry alligator is going to look for a second helping.

And you look pretty tasty.

So you're a second helping. But don't take it too hard! After all, you aways did like helping others.

In fact, there's a name for a kid like you.

Gator-aid!

THE END

It's still dark, so the zombies can't see you clearly. You step out from behind the tree.

"UUUURRRGGHH!" you moan in your best zombie imitation.

"So the last hiker is now one of us," Krump gloats.

"Fooo," you moan. You wonder for a moment if there's an Oscar for the Best Imitation of an Undead Fiend.

If there were, you wouldn't win it. Coach Krump peers suspiciously at you. "You look a little too healthy," he says. "To be on the safe side, I'd better spray you again."

Spray you? Your eyes go wide with horror.

Coach Krump raises his water gun.

One drop and you're dead — worse than dead!

But Uncle Ed darts from behind the tree and grabs the gun!

"It's all over, Cemetery Man!" Uncle Ed calls. "You'll never turn another kid into a zombie!"

"Nooooo!" Coach Krump shrieks.

The two men struggle for the water gun. You watch helplessly as they sway back and forth. Is Uncle Ed winning?

Suddenly, liquid jets out from the water gun.

And hits . . .

Hits who? Find out on PAGE 34.

"Let's go back down the tunnel," you whisper to Pat. "It's too risky to go through the kitchen. There was a turnoff a little way back. Let's see where it goes."

"I didn't like it in the tunnel," Pat whines. "I'd rather go through the kitchen."

You think for a moment. "Okay, let me check out the turnoff. If I find a way out, I'll come back for you."

You head back down the tunnel. At the turnoff, you enter a drainpipe. Water sloshes around your sneakers. The air stinks.

Soon the main pipe breaks into two smaller pipes. Much smaller. You enter the right-hand pipe on your hands and knees.

Suddenly, a strong rush of water knocks you down.

"Help!" you shout. Your cry ends in a gurgle as you're sucked underwater.

You barrel on down the pipe.

Where will you come out?

Tumble to PAGE 82.

"Later," you tell Kim. "I'm hiking by myself."

You strap your sleeping bag to your backpack, stick your water bottle in your pocket, and start off down the trail.

The other kids are already ahead of you. But you don't mind. It's a great day for a walk in the woods.

Up ahead, Zombie Mountain is in view. The top is sharp and craggy. But it doesn't look too steep.

As you tramp through the woods, the trail twists and turns. You come to a fork in the road. You choose the branch that turns toward the mountain. After an hour, you reach another fork.

You listen for other hikers. All you hear are birds singing.

Which way should you go?

You reach in your pack for your map. You study it, searching for the trail you're on.

Hey. What's going on?

This map is totally confusing. There are *three* trails on it. And none of them looks like the one you're on.

You're lost!

Try to find your way to PAGE 109.

Coach Rex points to a large ant farm on his desk. Pasted on it is a handwritten label. It says CAMP FARM.

Coach Rex lovingly pats his ant farm and waves at the little occupants.

"See the ants doing their job?" he barks at you. "They don't talk back. And they don't have food fights."

You nod your head numbly.

"This camp is like the ant farm. And the campers are like ants. Do I make myself clear?"

You think: Earth to Coach Rex. Kids aren't ants! But out loud, you say, "Crystal clear, Coach Rex."

"I'm sorry, but you are not Selection material," Coach Rex declares. "But we'll see how you do as a team player."

Oh, man! It's only your first day at Camp Running Leaf, and already you've been axed from the Selection!

What a bummer!

You leave Coach Rex gazing at his ant farm and slink back to the cafeteria.

Get going to PAGE 51.

"We'll follow the river," you declare.

You and Kim set out along the bank. The river flows swiftly next to you. Zombie Mountain stands tall above you. It would be a perfect hike, you think — if it weren't for Kim.

"My feet hurt," she complains. She punches you in the shoulder. "This was your dumb idea!"

The path starts getting muddy. "I'm ruining my new sneakers!" Kim whines.

"Tough," you reply. What a baby! you think.

The path grows muddier and gunkier. And Kim's complaints grow louder and more obnoxious. She starts blaming you for the slow going.

Please, you think, let us reach Zombie Cave. Soon!

Your thoughts are cut off by Kim's terrified scream.

Quick! Turn to PAGE 83!

Why go for a boring old rib when you could impress all the other hikers with a skull?

You place your hands around the skeleton's head. A shiver runs along your spine.

You're holding a human skull in your hands!

Slowly, gently, you begin to pull. At first nothing happens.

Then, suddenly, the skull pops off the neck bones.

And begins to vibrate in your hands!

"What's happening?" Kim cries.

"I don't know!" you exclaim.

A red glow appears in the skull's bony eye sockets.

Then its jaw moves. And it begins to speak!

"Many thanks!" it booms.

You nearly drop the skull. "Are — are you alive?" you gasp.

"I was once," the skull replies. "An evil spell made me into what I am now."

"Who cast the spell?" you ask, wide-eyed.

"The person I replaced. He left me here to guard the cave. My freedom comes only when someone else takes *my* place."

Takes his place?

"What do you mean?" you demand.

Go on to PAGE 66 — if you can handle it!

18

Kim comes up behind you. "What's wrong?" she asks.

"A-a zombie!" you stammer.

"Oh, please," Kim snaps. "I mean, do I look that stupid?"

You'd like to answer that question. But you're speechless. Because the creature in the cave is the nastiest thing you've ever seen. Gashes cover its colorless face. Its eyes are dead.

It *smells* dead!

"No!" you cry. "It really *is* a zombie!"

The thing takes several steps toward you. "UUURRGH!" it moans.

"Eeeeeeeeee!" Kim screams.

"Sorry — we . . . uh . . . we took a wrong turn," you tell the undead monster. You begin backing out the way you came.

The zombie staggers toward you.

"Run!" you order Kim.

The zombie lumbers along after you. It doesn't run fast. But it doesn't tire, either. How can you escape? you wonder frantically. Then you have an idea.

"Climb up the cliff!" you shout at Kim.

"Are you crazy?" she cries. "It's a *cliff*!"

"Would you rather get caught by the zombie?" you ask.

Enough said! The two of you start scrambling up the cliff.

Scramble up to PAGE 80.

Desperately, you try to think of a way out.

That's when you remember the old man down the road. The one who gave you directions to the camp.

He might let you use his phone. The trouble is, it's the middle of the night. Can you convince him to let you in?

You snap your fingers as you remember something else. The old man said there was a gas station near the camp. A gas station would probably have a pay phone. You could call Uncle Ed from there.

You dash up the driveway leading out of the camp. Out to the main road.

Now you have to decide: Should you go right to the service station, or left to the old man's house?

Which way do you turn?

If you try to get help from the old man, turn to PAGE 84.

If you go to the service station, turn to PAGE 24.

"I'll guard the goal for a while," you tell Antoine.

Antoine glares at you and stalks away.

The soccer game starts again. The powerful players kick rockets. You hope your defense keeps the ball away from you.

But they don't. A kid from the other team breaks free and takes a shot — *BOOM!*

No way are you going to try to stop *that*. You dive out of the way of the speeding ball.

It tears the net in half!

The soccer coach, Goodrich, comes running over. "Your job is to stop the ball — even if it kills you!"

"Death by soccer kick?" You laugh. "No way!"

You glance around. Whoa. No one else is laughing.

"Okay," you promise. "I'll stop the next shot."

But you don't stop the next one, or the one after that. Some of the shots whiz by so fast, you never even see them. Finally Coach Goodrich tosses you out of the game and calls back Antoine.

You slink back to your bunk.

So maybe you're not quite ready for the World Cup.

Dribble to PAGE 91.

"Fooooo!" the zombies groan. "UUUU-URGGGHHHH!"

"What do they want?" Kim asks in a trembling whisper.

"I think they want to eat us," you whisper back.

The zombies circle you. Their putrid flesh smells like a combination of rotten eggs and car exhaust — only stronger. "UUUUURGH!" they moan. "FOOOOOO! UUURGH!"

The one-armed zombie reaches toward you. A worm slithers over his oozing, rotting palm.

"No!" you scream. You swat his arm away.

SPLUMP! The arm falls right off his shoulder! It hits the ground with a sound like a wet sponge.

"UUUURGH!" he bellows. The other zombies press closer. And now they sound angry too.

Great move. Now you're *really* in trouble.

Think fast. You have no weapons. And besides, what could kill a thing that's already dead?

Wait! You have that survival kit. The one Krump gave you at the start of the hike. You have no idea what it contains.

There might be something in there that could help you.

Or you might waste precious time checking it out.

See what's in the survival kit on PAGE 92.
Try to fight your way out on PAGE 85.

The alligator is sitting on a rock in the middle of the lake, trying to get the crowbar out of its mouth.

"So what?" Brad smirks. "You still lost the race."

Coach Karla peers at the alligator. You expect her to call in an alligator catcher immediately. Or at least look shocked.

But instead, she does some calculations on her clipboard.

Then she raises your arm in the air. "You get bonus points for the alligator. That means you tied with Brad for first!"

Your mouth falls open. Is she kidding?

Coach Rex claps you on the shoulder. "Good work fighting that alligator."

You finally find your voice. "Good work?" you sputter. "How can you let kids swim in a gator-infested swamp?"

Coach Rex's smile fades. He gives you a chilling glare. "Just get ready for the next event!"

You and Brad walk into the stadium. Dozens of campers watch silently from the stands.

Coach Rex strides right behind you. You hear him tell one of the other coaches, "Watch those two. I have a feeling they didn't eat the eggs."

You shiver. Now you want to win the bike more than ever — so you can escape from this horrible camp!

Turn to PAGE 7.

You wait for the workers to leave the kitchen.

Because of that, you see something you wish you hadn't.

The blue-skinned worker places a plastic tube in the hole on top of his head. Slowly, blue fluid begins to seep down the tube. The fluid flows out the tube and into the vat.

So that's what makes the eggs blue!

Alien brain fluid!

Gross!

After the vat is refilled, the blue-skinned worker coils the tube and puts it in a drawer. Then all the cooks troop out of the kitchen by the far door.

"Now's our chance!" you exclaim.

Cautiously, you open the door to the kitchen.

The coast looks clear.

You make your dash.

But just as you reach the doors, someone barges through them going the other way. The swinging doors knock you and Pat flat on your backs.

Uh-oh! Better go to PAGE 100.

You cut right on the road, making for the service station. In the distance, you hear the sounds of the campers searching for you. You hear Coach Rex screaming, "Find that traitor!"

Oh, no! If Coach Rex gets hold of you, you'll end up in the infirmary. The place of no return!

Thank goodness! There's the gas station. And there's the pay phone. You search your pockets for a quarter. You can't find one!

That's okay, you can call collect.

Uncle Ed answers the phone groggily. "Wha — ?" he mumbles.

When you relate the story, he sounds disbelieving.

"I mean it, Uncle Ed," you insist. "Camp Running Leaf — hah! It should be called Camp Run-for-Your-Life!"

"All right, all right. I'll come get you," Uncle Ed promises. "Just wait out in front of the gas station."

As soon as you hang up the phone, you hide in the back of the station. The searchers are coming closer.

Peeking around the corner, you see them. An army of glassy-eyed kids.

"Hurry, Uncle Ed," you whisper. "Hurry!"

Turn to PAGE 89.

Coach Krump is gone!

You glance back at the person with the water gun. He's now bent over Kim. The embers of the campfire give off just enough light for you to see his face.

It's Coach Krump!

Coach Krump is the one making your friends into zombies.

And now he's moving toward *your* sleeping bag!

You've got to get out of this nightmare! You scuttle toward the woods. But a voice calls out, "UUURGHHH!"

It's Kim. Only Kim is now a zombie. She stands by the fire. Her eyes are lifeless. Flies buzz around her putrid flesh.

She points straight at you. "FOOO!"

Time to boogie.

You zig through the trees. You zag through the bushes.

In the distance, you hear Coach Krump shouting, "Head for Camp Running Leaf! We'll get the rest of them there!"

You'd like to warn the campers. Except there's no way you can find your way back to camp. Unless you follow the zombies.

It seems risky. Maybe you should just run away.

To follow the zombies to camp, turn to PAGE 135.

To run as far from the zombies as possible, go to PAGE 56.

Unfortunately, Brad is also a star gymnast. A hotshot.

Without even breaking a sweat, he pulls a 9.9 too.

You're still tied for first place.

You expect the audience of campers to send up a big cheer. But they're all moving silently to the exits. The stadium loudspeaker blares a message: "All campers not in the Selection, report to the infirmary immediately."

"Why are they going to the infirmary?" you ask one of the coaches.

"Just a routine check for, uh, poison ivy," she answers.

All at once? You're confused. "How can such a small building hold so many people?" you demand.

"No time for chitchat," Coach Rex barks, striding up to you. "Next up is the javelin."

You follow him to the javelin pit. But what you see makes you feel like forfeiting.

Get the point on PAGE 8.

You want to move that runner to second. So you drop down a good sacrifice bunt.

"Way to go," cheers the coach.

You smile. Then you hear him say, "You must be eating your eggs. Be sure to eat them three times a day."

What's the story? you wonder. Why are the coaches pushing eggs on every camper?

Over the loudspeaker, the bugle sounds. Like clockwork, all the kids drop their balls and gloves and march to the cafeteria. They move like robots, you think.

The lunch menu: blue omelette sandwiches. This time you just hide yours in your napkin. Pat gobbles his down.

Doo-doo doot-a-doot, doo-doo doot-a-doot! There goes that bugle again. Everyone jumps up and runs back out to the fields.

"C'mon," calls Pat. "You mustn't be late for an activity."

You stare at Pat, puzzled. When did he turn into such a stickler for rules?

One minute, he was normal. Then . . .

Wait! Didn't he change after eating the eggs?

Turn to PAGE 98.

"Later, Kim!" you call. With a burst of speed, you dash down the trail.

You look fearfully over your shoulder. The zombie has stopped chasing you. It's bending over Kim.

Poor Kim.

Now she's really got something to complain about!

But you've got your own problems. The main one being, it's five minutes to midnight and no campsite is in sight.

Four minutes . . .

You keep running. Still no sign of the camp.

Three minutes . . .

You can barely see the trail. You aim your flashlight down the path. But the batteries go dead!

It's midnight. No way are you going to get that medal now.

Besides which, you're alone in a forest full of zombies.

You're lost. The only thing you can do is lay down your sleeping bag and wait for morning to come.

Camp for the night on PAGE 131.

Is Coach Rex really saying what you think he's saying?

That you went through the whole, horrible Selection just so you could become a slave to an alien overlord?

And die a gruesome death?

"Come on," Coach Rex booms. "Time to transport you!"

You're in a tight spot. But you don't give up easily.

You've got one last chance to save yourself. If only you can get to that mountain bike. . . .

You leap off the victory platform and race to the cafeteria.

Coach Rex runs after you. "There is no escape," he shouts.

Unfortunately, he's right.

The mountain bike is gone.

Someone stole it. And that person is now pedaling it furiously across the stadium grass.

It's Brad! He's leaving Camp Run-for-Your-Life.

So are you. For an all-expenses-paid, lifetime vacation to Xentron.

Luckily for you, a slave's lifetime is mercifully short!

THE END

You've got to try the pole vault, you decide. You might not get another chance to escape.

Casually, you start toward the water fountain. It happens to be right next to the vaulting pole. "I'm just getting a drink," you call to Coach Rex.

You jog up to the fountain. When you're sure no one is looking, you seize the long pole. You back up a few yards, balancing the pole in your hands.

Then you start your run toward the stadium wall.

"Hey!" Coach Rex bellows. "Where are you going? Somebody stop that kid!"

But he's too late. You have already planted your pole in the soft ground by the wall. You leap into the air.

Up you soar, clutching the pole. Up, up. The stadium wall rushes toward you.

Will you clear it?

Or will you splat against it like a runny blue egg?

Get your results on PAGE 38.

Coach Krump wheels around and stands obediently before Uncle Ed. The zombie kids follow.

You let out your breath.

Yes! It worked!

The next day, Uncle Ed drives you to Camp Pendleton. The *real* Camp Pendleton.

"Maybe this time I'll win a medal," you say as you climb out of the car.

"Maybe, kid. Oh, before I forget — I have something for you." Uncle Ed hands you a slip of pale green paper.

"What's this?" you ask, mystified.

"It's a check," Uncle Ed replies. "Didn't I tell you? There's a reward for capturing the Cemetery Man."

You peer down at the check. Your eyes bulge. You've never seen so many zeroes!

As it turns out, you don't win any medals at Camp Pendleton. But you don't care. Because now you can *buy* all the medals you want!

THE END

You reach down and break off the skeleton's cracked rib.

A moment later, the rest of the bones crumble to dust!

"We got the bone!" Kim crows.

"Yeah," you mutter. You wish you could feel excited. But you're too creeped out. You just want to get out of here.

You glance at your watch. 11:00 P.M. One hour to find the campsite!

You and Kim hurry out of the cave. Kim examines her map by flashlight. "This way," she calls, heading downhill.

She seems confident about where she's going. So you follow her. The moon is up, but it's still very dark in the trees.

After a few moments you come to a place where the trees are thinner. The ground seems strangely rocky.

"Come on," Kim orders, beckoning impatiently.

You're halfway across the rocky field when you stumble over something. You shine your flashlight down to see what it was.

Whoa. It's not a rock. It's a gravestone.

You're in a graveyard!

Turn to PAGE 137.

The nurse, a bone-thin woman with a knobby bun, shrugs. "I've done the repairs, but I'm still not certain how well the transporter is working."

"Well, let's use this one as a guinea pig," Coach Rex suggests, pointing at you.

"All right. Just step this way, dear," the nurse coos. She steers you onto a large steel platform. "This won't hurt at all."

Your head whips back and forth between Coach Rex and the nurse. "Wh-what are you going to do to me?" you stammer.

Coach Rex tells you, "If you make it to Xentron, there's no reason you can't work the mines. I'm sure you'll last as long as the average slave: three years."

"What's Xentron? What mines?" you demand, terrified.

Then, from above, a blue light sweeps over your body.

You feel a tingling. Whoa! Coach Rex, the nurse, the infirmary — they're all fading from sight!

You're really being transported. Just like in the movies!

Unfortunately, the transporter *isn't* working right. Instead of sending you to Xentron, it beams you directly into the sun. In seconds, you're so hot Coach Rex could fry a blue egg on your head!

But hey, it could be worse. At least you'll get a tan this summer!

THE END

34

Uncle Ed turns around. His eyes are bulging. Coach Krump also turns around. His eyes are . . .

Dead.

Coach Krump has become a zombie!

He moans, "Fooo!" and heads straight for you.

"Get out of the way!" Uncle Ed shouts to you. He holds up the water gun. "I'm the master now, Krump. Do my bidding."

Krump turns to stare at Uncle Ed, drooling.

You hold your breath. Your heart pounds.

Can Uncle Ed really control the zombies?

Go to PAGE 31.

Someone is bending over the sleeping Tracy.

Aiming a gun at her!

You're about to shout a warning. Then you see something that makes you laugh.

The gun squirts liquid on her.

It's only a water gun!

But Tracy sits bolt upright, screaming. Then her eyes film over. Her face seems to shrivel. She moans softly. "Uurrgghh . . ."

You've heard that moan before.

Tracy has turned into a zombie!

Something in that water gun is transforming the living into the living dead!

The person with the water gun creeps over to Ted's sleeping bag. He squirts the liquid in Ted's face.

Ted wakes with a moan. He rises, hands outstretched.

This is awful! All your fellow hikers are becoming zombies!

You'd better wake Coach Krump. Maybe he'll know what to do.

Quietly, you unzip your sleeping bag. You crawl around the campfire to where Coach is sleeping.

But his sleeping bag is empty!

Quick! Turn to PAGE 25.

You know the person running toward the shack. Her name is Kim. She goes to your school back home. You've disliked her since you did a geography project together. Kim complained the whole time. Even worse — *you* had to do all the work.

"I don't believe this!" she exclaims when she catches sight of you. "Of all the camps in the whole country, I end up at the same one as you."

Great. She's already complaining! you think.

A pale, heavyset man in a white shirt comes puffing up.

"I'm Coach Krump," he says. "Okay, listen up, campers. The point of the hike is to earn your Outdoors Medal."

He reaches in his pocket and pulls out a shiny disk. "This is the medal," he says. He holds it up.

It gleams in the sunshine as if made of gold. A small figure is carved on it. You can't quite make out what it is.

"Cool," you murmur. You reach for the medal to examine it more closely.

Coach Krump snatches it away.

"Hands off!" he thunders.

Go on to PAGE 52.

Take a deep breath, because you're about to dive into the stinky muck!

You double up and head for the bottom. At first, you can't see anything. The muddy water hurts your eyes. But when you get a few feet below the surface, the water clears.

There's no sign of the kid who went down. You look all around. Nothing.

But, wait! There's something lying at the bottom of the lake. Something white. You swim in for a closer look.

Teeth grin up at you.

Whoa.

It's a skull!

A human skull!

Swim on to PAGE 116.

The sides of your sneakers brush the stadium wall as you sail over it.

You made it!

You escaped from Camp Run-for-Your-Life!

You hit the ground running. And you don't slow down until you're miles away, deep in the woods. Where no one can find you.

You'd like to call Uncle Ed, but you don't have any quarters in your gym shorts. So you're forced to walk. Luckily, you remember that your friend Colleen just moved to a town only a few miles away from the camp. You're pretty sure you can find it.

You reach Colleen's house the next morning, hungry and exhausted. Colleen's parents have already gone to work. She's home alone. And boy, is she surprised to see you!

"Want some scrambled eggs?" she offers.

You shudder. You'll never eat eggs again!

"So what happened to you?" Colleen demands as you devour peanut butter and jelly sandwiches in her kitchen. "I thought you were going to some great sports camp. Didn't you like it?"

You swallow a bite of sandwich and wash it down with milk.

"Let me put it this way," you say at last. "Next summer, I'm going to a computer camp!"

THE END

"FOOD FIGHT!" you bellow.

You stand up and fling a handful of blue eggs at the kid across the table. They splat all over his face. Pat flips his toast like a Frisbee at another kid. You both laugh.

Without warning, a big hand grabs you by the collar.

Uh-oh! It's Coach Rex!

Veins bulge in his forehead. "Come with me," he growls.

Coach Rex takes you from the cafeteria to his office.

"So you're messing with the eggs," he snarls. "Throwing around vital nourishment."

"No!" you gasp. "I was just having fun."

You blink. You can almost see steam coming from Coach Rex's ears.

"Let me show you something," he says. "I think you'll find it very interesting."

What could be more interesting than blue eggs? Turn to PAGE 15 to find out.

40

You get your pile of eggs, topped by toast. As you search for an empty seat, you see someone you know from home.

"Hey, Pat!" you exclaim.

You sit down next to a thin, fast-talking kid. He lives a few blocks from you. You're glad to see a familiar face.

"Hi," Pat answers. "I just got here a couple of days ago. Most of the kids have already been here a few weeks."

He hasn't touched his eggs. He tells you, "I'm not hungry."

You notice he looks kind of sick. He's pale. And his eyes have dark circles under them.

"Well, I'm starved," you announce.

You plunge your fork into your eggs and lift it up to your mouth.

Your hand suddenly freezes.

Whoa!

The egg yolks are *blue*.

Turn to PAGE 10.

You race back past the snake pit and snatch the javelin out of Coach Rex's hands.

You dart back to Brad's side. Hooking the point of the javelin under the rattlesnake's body, you lift the furious reptile away from Brad. You toss it back into the pit. It writhes and hisses angrily.

Then you hold the javelin out to Brad. "Grab hold," you command, and pull him to his feet.

You're a hero. But does Brad thank you for saving him?

No way! Instead, he shoves you to the ground.

"Eat my dust, sucker!" he sneers. Then he sprints down the track and crosses the finish line. What a jerk!

"We have a winner!" Coach Rex cries. He holds Brad's arm aloft. Brad is led to the victory platform.

You stand on the track. Now what are you going to do? Brad won the special prize — the mountain bike. The mountain bike that was your hope for escaping Camp Run-for-Your-Life.

Are you trapped here?

If you really want to know, turn to PAGE 43.

42

You lie on the bunk, thinking about your first day in camp. At first, you only hear your bunk mates snoring.

Then you hear a voice. A voice you know well: Coach Rex. He's talking to another coach as they make the rounds of the cabins.

And what they're saying makes your blood run cold.

"This is a pretty good crop of specimens," Rex is saying.

"Is the transporter ready?" asks the other.

"As soon as we fix the wormhole lens unit," Coach Rex answers.

Specimens?

Transporter?

Wormhole lens unit?

What are they talking about?

Find out more on PAGE 88.

Coach Rex's voice booms over the loudspeaker. "Congratulations, camper!" he tells Brad.

Yeah, yeah, you think glumly.

Then you hear Coach Rex's next words. And a shiver shakes your entire body.

"In a few minutes, you will be transported from the infirmary to the planet Xentron," Coach Rex announces. "There you will have the honor of being the Overmaster's slave. After you've served him for a period of time, he will serve you — for dinner!"

Your jaw drops. So *that*'s the special prize! Going to an alien planet as a slave! And then getting eaten!

You thought this kind of thing only happened in movies. Horror movies!

Then you have a terrible thought.

What is second prize?

Uh-oh. You've got to get out of here, before Coach Rex turns his attention to *you*.

But how?

Then an idea pops into your head.

Turn to PAGE 93 to find out more about your idea.

44

You slip inside and shut the door. Slowly, silently, you creep through the dark hall.

EEEee-EEEee-EEEee! A weird, high, pulsing sound drifts through an open door.

You peek around the edge of the doorway. Steps. Going down — to the cellar, probably.

Your heart thuds as you pad down the steps. There's another door at the bottom. The pulsing sound is coming from behind it.

You slowly open the door.

What you see makes your eyes bug out!

The room inside looks like NASA mission control! People in headphones stride back and forth from radar screens to electronic maps. "We've got an interstellar–Camp Running Leaf linkup," someone is yelling.

"Wow!" you gasp aloud.

Big mistake.

Find out why on PAGE 104.

"You be the zombie," you tell Uncle Ed. "After all, you're the secret agent."

You and Uncle Ed track the Cemetery Man and his army to a clearing near Camp Running Leaf.

"Hide behind this tree until I give you the signal," Uncle Ed whispers.

Then he lurches into the middle of the clearing, moaning.

You peek around the tree. Isn't Uncle Ed getting a little too close to the zombie campers?

Before you can warn him, Samantha darts over and bites him on the leg. "Fooo," she moans.

Uncle Ed shudders. His eyes instantly glaze over.

His skin turns ashy and starts to curl away from his bones.

Guess what?

He's not *pretending* to be a zombie any longer.

Uncle Ed spins and points to your hiding place. "Foooo!" he moans.

The zombies stalk toward you. Horrified, you turn and run.

But before you get very far, you feel something wet hit the back of your neck.

Oh, nooooo . . .

Are you brave enough to turn around on PAGE 130?

"What's the matter now?" you ask.

"It's nearly sunset," Kim whines. "And we're nowhere near Zombie Cave. It's your fault. You picked the wrong route."

You realize you might not make it to the camp-site by midnight.

You've got to move faster!

You gaze at the river, wondering what to do. Then you spot something that might solve your problem.

Just ahead, a small green rowboat is hauled up on the bank. A sign on the boat says PRIVATE PROPERTY.

"If we row, we'll reach the other side of the mountain in no time," you tell Kim.

"The boat doesn't belong to us," she objects. "If we get in trouble, it'll be your fault."

"Fine," you snap. You'd almost rather go to jail than listen to Kim whine for one more minute!

"Besides," Kim adds, "the map says there are rapids ahead."

Rapids? That could be a *real* problem.

What are you going to do?

To take the boat anyway, go to PAGE 9.
Continue on foot on PAGE 72.

A freshly risen zombie staggers toward you.

"Fooo!" it groans. "FOOO!"

Finally you get what it's saying.

FOOD. As in — you!

You're in a total terror meltdown.

A zombie grabs you. You knock its hand away. Another has Kim down. It's about to bite her!

You tackle the monster and pull it off her. Your fingers sink deep into the rotten flesh of its arm. Yecch!

"Run!" you scream. You and Kim sprint out of the graveyard.

The zombie's heavy footsteps thud behind you.

Then Kim trips over a tree root. She hits the ground hard. "Noooo!" she shrieks. "Help me! I hurt my ankle! Help me!"

The zombie is only a few feet away. You know that if you were hurt, Kim would leave you hanging.

So should *you* stick your neck out for *her*?

Help Kim on PAGE 102
Or keep running to PAGE 28.

"A zombie!" Kim shrieks.

"What are you talking about?" a familiar voice cries.

It's Coach Krump! You practically faint with relief.

"Where have you been?" the coach demands. "It's almost midnight."

You start to tell him about the zombies, but the coach waves you off. "Camp's just over this ridge," he tells you. "Didn't you see the sign?" He points to a white sign that says CAMP-OUT.

You follow him to the campsite. The other kids are already in their sleeping bags, snoring.

"Isn't there any food? I'm starving," Kim complains.

"You missed the cookout," the coach replies. He doesn't seem to care that you're both hungry. "It's time to sleep."

"How about our medals?" you ask. "We're the only ones who got a bone from Zombie Cave."

"We'll talk about it tomorrow!" Coach Krump snaps. "Now turn in."

What a grouch!

You crawl into your sleeping bag. You're just dozing off when a noise awakens you. You glance across the campfire . . .

And feel your heart stop in fear.

Go on to PAGE 35.

"Coach Krump is the Cemetery Man?" you gasp.

What does it all mean?

Uncle Ed lays his hand on your shoulder. "Listen carefully. We don't have much time," he warns. "You see, the Cemetery Man is a chemist. He — well, to put it simply, he developed a chemical that will bring the dead back to life. The thing is, his formula has a horrible side effect. One drop on the skin will turn living humans temporarily into zombies!"

You remember Coach Krump's water gun. And the beaker in the cemetery. They must have held the zombie-making chemical!

You stare at Uncle Ed in horror. "But why?" you blurt. "Why is he making all these zombies?"

"He's creating an army," Uncle Ed explains. "The zombies are completely under his control. We think he plans to take over the world!"

"He sounds completely insane," you whisper.

"He is," Uncle Ed agrees. "And it's my job to stop him." He gazes solemnly at you. "But I need your help."

Flip to PAGE 123.

"What happens if we're late?" you ask.

"Are the zombies going to get us?" Al adds, grinning.

"They might." The coach glares at Al. "Or they could just as easily get you earlier. But if you're late, you're disqualified. No Outdoors Medal for you."

"We won't be late," you all chorus.

"You'll be safer hiking in pairs," Krump calls. "As soon as you've chosen partners, start the hike. See you at the campsite!"

You see that Samantha has already paired up with Al. Ted and Tracy are starting up the trail together.

That leaves you with . . . Kim?

No way! you think. She's lazy. She's a complainer. Besides, you're a good hiker. You don't need a partner.

On the other hand, Coach Krump told you to pair up.

What will you do?

.

To pair up with Kim, go to PAGE 118.
To hike alone, turn to PAGE 14.

As you slide back into your seat at the cafeteria, you notice that Pat's lips are covered with blue egg.

"I thought you weren't going to eat your eggs," you say.

Pat shrugs. "One of the coaches made me. They're pretty good." He smiles weakly. His eyes look a little glazed.

Another camper, Charlie, comes over. He's about your height. But he's very muscular.

Come to think of it, all the campers look strong.

But, hey, this *is* a sports camp.

In a monotone, Charlie says, "I loved food fights at school. But" — he scratches his head, as if trying to remember something — "we must eat our eggs, not throw them."

Another camper shuffles over. "Yeah," he chimes in. "We're supposed to follow the rules."

You roll your eyes. What's wrong with these kids? Haven't they ever heard of having a little fun? You're beginning to think this place *is* like an ant farm. Everyone acts like they're in the army!

You're not sure you can hack this place. Maybe you should pretend to be sick and call Uncle Ed to pick you up.

On the other hand, what if Uncle Ed thinks you're a wimp?

Maybe you should just stick it out.

If you pretend to be sick, turn to PAGE 79.
If you stick it out, turn to PAGE 58.

"I just wanted to see the medal," you gasp, shocked.

"Not till you've completed the hike!" Coach Krump bellows. He leans over. "Understand?" he says, right in your face.

This guy is weird, you think. You wonder if you've made the wrong choice.

"To earn your medals, you must be able to read a map and get around in the wilderness," Coach Krump goes on. He holds up a map and points to a mountain. "You must find Zombie Cave, here on Zombie Mountain, and remove a bone from it as proof you were there."

Zombie Mountain? Excellent. You love spooky stuff.

"A bone?" Kim exclaims. "Ewwwww!"

"The cave is full of bones," Coach Krump declares. "Human bones," he adds with a smile.

Now he passes out maps, one to each kid. "After you leave Zombie Cave," he continues, "we'll all meet at the campsite on Zombie Mountain."

Cool, you think. First a spooky fossil hunt, then a camp-out. This is going to be great!

"One more thing," Coach Krump adds. He glares from camper to camper. "Watch out for zombies."

What? *Turn to PAGE 132.*

"I'll play forward instead," you volunteer. "The goalie can keep his job if he really wants it."

The rest of the team agrees. You jog onto the field.

PHWEEEET! The soccer coach, Goodrich, blows a whistle. And the game starts again.

Soon you're wishing you'd agreed to tend goal. It might have been a little easier.

You were the star player on your soccer team at home. But these kids have legs of iron. They don't play like humans. They play like maniacs!

When the coach tells them to execute, nothing stops them. You can't knock them off the ball. And their bullet shots and passes force you to duck.

This is the first time you've ever been *scared* in a soccer game.

By the time it's over, you're completely bushed. You drag yourself back to your cabin and collapse on your bunk.

Turn to PAGE 91.

A hungry mountain lion can move a lot faster than a hungry zombie, you reason. Better take your chances with the corpse.

"Up!" you order Kim.

You scramble back up the cliff. Rocks and pebbles rain down around you.

"Uurrgghh!" the zombie bellows from above. You peer up. It hefts another huge boulder. Oh, no! How can it miss when you're this close?

Then the zombie slips!

"UUUURRRRRGGGHHH!" it cries as it tumbles through the air. Down, down, down.

It lands with a sickening *THUD* far, far below. Yuck!

"Wow, Kim," you comment as you reach the top of the cliff. "That zombie really fell for you."

"Hah, hah," Kim huffs.

Time to check out the cave. You hike down the trail and stand nervously at the entrance. A faint light glows from inside.

You take a deep breath.

"Let's do it," you say to Kim. "Let's enter Zombie Cave."

Well, go on! Enter the cave on PAGE 126.

The yellow eyes are coming toward you —
FAST!

They're just a few feet away. That's when you
see a long green snout.

A snout that opens to reveal dozens of long,
jagged teeth.

An alligator!

Think fast! What are you going to do?

Do you have time to do a frog kick and get
away?

Or should you grab the crowbar and try to de-
fend yourself?

Whatever you do, you'd better do it *now*!

If you do the frog kick, turn to PAGE 107.
If you grab the crowbar, turn to PAGE 108.

56

Keep running, you say to yourself. Sooner or later, you're bound to find the camp. Or a road. Or a town.

Or *something* besides zombies!

You crash through the dark woods. All you care about is escaping.

Finally, you spot something white ahead. A sign.

It reads: CAMP-OUT.

Oh, no! You're back at the camp-out site! You ran in big circles!

You stumble to a halt, panting.

SNAP! A branch breaks.

Then you feel breathing on your neck.

Someone — or some*thing* — is right behind you!

It's too late to hide. Slowly, you turn around.

Face it on PAGE 87.

You and Brad line up, side by side.

"What do you think they have planned for us?" you whisper.

Brad shrugs. "I guess we'll find out," he whispers back. "Just remember, we're in this together. You help me, I help you."

Sounds good to you. But you notice that Brad doesn't meet your eyes. Can you trust him?

The starting gun goes off, and you sprint out. As you approach the first hurdle, you're in the lead. Barely.

You take off over the water jump. Up, up, up you go.

As you come down, your heel slaps against the water's edge. A tiny bit of the liquid splashes on your calf.

"OUCH!" You scream in pain. That stuff burns!

"Don't let a little sulfuric acid slow you down!" Coach Rex bellows at you.

Acid? This is insane! You gaze desperately around. Any chance you could veer off the course and run to safety?

Not much. The whole track is surrounded by the coaches. So escape isn't likely. Just finish the race and get your prize.

The next obstacle is approaching. You leap up, balance for a moment on top of the hurdle, and peer down at the pool.

You wish you hadn't!

To find out why, turn to PAGE 69.

58

"So," you ask Pat, pretending everything is normal. "What's the first sport of the day?"

"Baseball," he answers in a dull voice.

Pat was always a little dull, you think. But now he's really drippy!

You follow him out to the baseball diamond. The coach chooses up sides. You play shortstop.

You ask the players to talk it up in the infield. No one does.

You ask them to talk it up in the dugout.

Silence.

Everyone is hitting the ball hard and playing well. But . . . is anyone out here having fun?

Finally, you're at bat.

You pop a weak one up to the second baseman. The next batter drones, "Coach told me to hit a homer. Must hit a homer."

Whoa! She knocks the first pitch right over the fence!

Now you *really* want to do well.

Next time around, the batter before you singles. The coach tells you to lay down a sacrifice bunt. But you get a fast pitch. Should you follow orders?

Or would you rather swing for the fences?

If you swing your hardest, go to PAGE 136.
If you bunt, go to PAGE 27.

You stop short. "Who are you?" you gasp.

"I'm the Cemetery Man," the tall figure informs you.

The Cemetery Man? The one Coach Krump said didn't exist?

Uh-oh . . .

You can't see his face in the darkness. But his deep, hoarse voice is somehow familiar. "Thanks for falling into my trap," he says, chuckling.

"T-t-trap?" you stammer.

"Yes. I set it up for my zombies," the Cemetery Man rasps. "You see, they love the taste of human flesh. Especially brains. They believe eating brains will make them smarter. Imagine — an army of intelligent zombies!"

"You can't let them eat our brains!" you cry.

"Can't I?" The Cemetery Man aims a remote control at the zombies' cage. He presses a button.

The door springs open!

The zombies lurch toward you. "Foo fo fawt!" they moan. "Foo fo fawt!"

As the zombies surround you and Kim, you finally figure out what they're saying:

"Food for thought! Food for thought!"

THE END

60

Your only hope is to row toward that streamlet on your left.

But the current is so powerful. Will you make it?

Only one way to find out. You hand one oar to Kim. "Row!" you shout to her. "Row on the right side of the boat!"

You dip your oar in the water on the right too. Together, you and Kim row as hard as you can. The boat begins to inch left, toward the little stream.

Up ahead, the falls rage. Closer. Closer. You glance at the white water and gulp.

If you go over, you'll be smashed into a million pieces!

"Harder!" you shout to Kim. "Row harder!"

You dig your oar into the water.

Now the falls are only a couple of feet away.

Are you going to make it to the little stream?

Or are you going over the edge?

You can't watch. You shut your eyes.

Turn to PAGE 129.

You turn left at the fork. That will take you back to the main trail.

You hope.

"Kim?" you call. "Kim, are you there?"

No answer.

The trail begins to climb. Soon, you're at the top of a steep cliff. You glance down at the sharp rocks below.

You step cautiously onto the narrow trail along the cliff. You edge around a big rock and continue slowly, hugging the cliff.

Then you hear a crunching sound. There's someone behind you!

It must be Kim, you think. You stop and wait for her to appear.

And then you gasp.

Whoever is coming isn't Kim. It's not even human.

You watch in horror as the thing begins to come around the bend.

All you can see are two long, sharp horns!

What is it? Take a peek on PAGE 67.

Already you can feel the heat from the flames.

Beside you, Brad makes a gulping noise. He stares at the flames with round eyes.

That's it. This camp is some kind of weird death trap! Pat was right. It *should* be called Camp Run-for-Your-Life!

"Brad!" you mutter. "We've got to do something."

"Maybe we can just run out of the stadium," he whispers.

"No way! Coach Rex is watching us like a hawk," you point out.

Brad snaps his fingers. "I've got it. We can both fake an injury during our routines."

"I'm not sure." You gnaw your lower lip. "We might be able to escape later."

"First gymnast!" the gymnastics coach yells.

"Your choice," Brad whispers.

"*Now,* camper!" Coach Rex bellows.

Time's up! Make your decision.

If you fake an injury during your routine, turn to PAGE 74.

If you go for the gusto and wait for a better chance to escape, turn to PAGE 122.

"Let's swim," you suggest to Pat.

"I hate swimming," Pat complains. "I'm going to do hurdles."

"Okay." You shrug. "Good luck."

Privately, you're a little relieved to see Pat go. He seems so gloomy. You're ready for some fun — and some sports!

The swimming coach, Karla, orders the swimmers to follow her. As you head to the water, a voice behind you calls out, "Hey, loser, get out of my way."

You turn around. It's that Brad kid. The other one who didn't eat the eggs. He struts past you.

"The gold is mine," he sneers. "The rest of you are just fighting for the silver."

Brad is one obnoxious dude. You don't much like him. But he's got spirit — unlike the other campers.

You think: Neither of us ate any blue eggs.

Is there a connection?

Brad's nose wrinkles as you get closer to the water. "What's that smell?" he demands.

Yuck! It smells like a giant dump of rotten eggs! What could be causing it?

Find out on PAGE 120.

You bring the fork to your mouth. Your lips close around the eggs.

WAIT A MINUTE!

Let's review the facts:

A. This is a GOOSEBUMPS book.

B. Those eggs are blue.

Now get serious. You should know better.

NEVER EAT BLUE EGGS IN A GOOSE-BUMPS BOOK!

Okay, if this is your first GOOSEBUMPS book, it's an honest mistake. But the rest of you should be ashamed of yourselves.

Spit those eggs out and go back to PAGE 10.

Whew! You stuck your landing.

The judges all hold up your scores: 9.9 — 9.9 — 9.9.

Yes!

You start to feel as if maybe Camp Running Leaf isn't so bad. Maybe the events are just... creative. Maybe you didn't *really* see a skull at the bottom of the lake. Maybe you should forget about escaping.

Maybe you should really go for that special prize....

See how Brad does on PAGE 26.

"Watch!" the skull commands.

As you stare in horror, the headless skeleton's fingers begin to twitch. Its arms move. The pile of bones stands up.

Then the space between its ribs begins to fill with organs!

First a red, bloody, beating heart appears. Then a slimy brown liver and red stomach. Wet, gray lungs inflate with air.

Muscles grow over the skeleton's bones. Then skin.

The skeleton is a living human being again!

It steps toward you, holding out its hand.

"Helllppp!" Kim screams, running from the cave.

You try to follow. But — your feet! They seem stuck to the floor. "No!" you plead. "No!"

Too late. As the former skeleton touches you, your skin crumbles and peels off. Your organs shrivel and fall out.

You're turning into a living skeleton!

The former skeleton snatches its head from your hands. Then it shoves you into the hole you dug. You fall, bones clattering.

"Guard the cave well," the skeleton orders. "And remember — if you want to get out of here, just use your head!"

THE END

You start to scream.

And then the rest of the creature appears.

You laugh in relief. It's only a mountain goat!

"BAAAAAAH!" it cries. It trots up and nuzzles your hand.

"BAAAAAAH yourself!" you tell it, laughing. "I don't have time to play with a goat!"

You turn around and continue along the steep trail. You glance back. The goat is following. "BAAAAH!" it bleats.

"Go away!" you order.

You hike on. The trail narrows even more.

You're so busy keeping your balance, you forget about the goat.

Until it butts you in the back.

And knocks you right over the edge of the cliff.

As you plunge toward the distant rocks below, you realize the sad truth.

You're a lousy hiker after all — no ifs, ands, or butts!

THE END

68

You still don't really know what the coaches are talking about. You only know it's something bad. Really bad.

You've got to get away!

But you can't leave just yet. Rex and the other coach are still chatting outside. You close your eyes and wait for your chance.

Will it ever come?

Well, that depends on what you did today. . . .

If you played goalie, turn to PAGE 99.
If you played forward, turn to PAGE 105.

There's nothing in the pool.

No water.

No acid.

Nothing.

It's a bottomless black hole.

"Watch out, loser!" Brad yells in your ear.

He balances beside you on top of the hurdle for a moment. Then he shoves off — and pushes you to one side.

"Whoa!" you shout, flailing your arms. You throw yourself off the hurdle.

But you're off balance. Your leap isn't long enough. You land half in and half out of the pit.

Your legs dangle over empty space.

Coach Rex runs up beside you along the track. "That pit goes three miles deep," he informs you. "And that's the hole truth."

You gasp, "Thanks for the info, Coach."

Quick, go to PAGE 128.

A javelin hurtles at your chest. You fling your-self to one side, then snap your hand out.

Yes! You snagged the wooden shaft!

So does Brad. Five other contestants also catch javelins. But not with their hands.

You've heard of the agony of defeat — but this is ridiculous!

I want *out*! you think. You don't care about winning anymore.

The losers are carried off to the infirmary. Just like all the other campers. You glance up at the stands.

There are less than a dozen people left. And they're all waiting in the long line for the infirmary!

"Ready for the final event?" Coach Rex calls cheerily.

As you turn back to him, your gaze is caught by a long pole leaning against the stadium wall. The kind they use in pole vaulting.

It looks long enough to clear the wall.

This could be your last chance to escape. But you've never pole-vaulted before. Can you make it over the wall?

Or should you hang in there, try to win the final event, and ride your mountain bike prize to safety?

If you try the pole vault, turn to PAGE 30.

If you go on to the final event, turn to PAGE 119.

You dig with your bare hands in the soft earth. Kim doesn't help. "I don't want to break a nail," she sniffs.

After digging down a few inches, you feel something hard. You paw feverishly at the dirt. Is it gold? Jewels?

Kim bends over for a look.

"It's a skeleton!" she gasps. "Human!"

You feel a chill. You thought Coach Krump was kidding when he said the cave was full of human bones. But it seems he was serious. Dead serious.

Swallowing your fear, you keep digging. Ten minutes later, you've uncovered the entire skeleton.

"Yuck! I'm not touching that thing!" Kim declares.

You're not eager to touch it, either. But you've got to get a bone if you're going to win the Outdoors Medal.

And after all you've been through, you *want* that medal!

"One of the ribs is cracked," Kim points out. "Break it off and take it."

You think it might be easier to lift off the skull. But on the other hand, the skull is bulky. It won't fit in your pack.

If you go for the skull, turn to PAGE 17.
If you go for the rib, go to PAGE 32.

That boat doesn't look sturdy enough for the rapids, you think. Besides, you really don't want to steal it. You could get in trouble. So you and Kim stick to the muddy trail.

A few minutes later, you spot another trail, leading away from the riverbank.

"This way!" you exclaim.

The trail leads straight toward the mountain. Instead of swamp mud, you're walking on grass.

"I told you we should go this way!" Kim cries. She pushes ahead of you.

Liar! you think. But you don't really care. Because at the end of the trail, you've spotted a dark hole.

It must be Zombie Cave!

"Hurry!" you urge Kim. "We're almost there!"

Kim speeds up. You speed up behind her. The trail is covered with soft moss and grass.

Kim takes another step — and disappears.

"Kim!" you yell. You rush up to where you last saw her. You step on the soft mossy surface.

Your foot goes right through.

You're falling!

Fall onto PAGE 75.

Pleased and happy, a zombie claps her newly mended hand on another's shoulder.

The mended hand falls off!

Oops! You're not as good a tailor as you thought.

One by one, all the other body parts you sewed on start falling off. The zombies slowly turn toward you.

Kim is trembling. "We've got to get out of here!"

"No way," you assure her. "I'm sure it will be okay. I just have to sew them up again."

"Yeah, sure. Later!" Kim mutters, and bolts away.

You hold up the needle and grin weakly at the approaching zombies. "Satisfaction guaranteed," you offer.

With a swipe, one zombie knocks the needle from your hand.

This does not look good.

Desperately, you begin, "I could try a different stitch —"

But the zombies don't let you finish your sentence. They surround you. Then they begin to tear *you* apart. Limb by limb.

Uh-oh. Your life is hanging by a thread.

SNIP!

THE END

"Let's fake injuries," you whisper quickly to Brad.

You take a deep breath and run toward the bar.

The flames are turned up as you jump for the bar. They roar from underground gas jets. Heat sears your feet right through your sneakers.

You start to swing around the bar. Flames lick at you.

Now you know how a barbecued chicken must feel!

You do a couple of practice twists. You're actually a good gymnast. It's hard for you to pretend to do badly, when you know you could be top dog.

But you've got to escape from Camp Run-for-Your-Life!

Okay, now's the time. Your plan is to let go of the bar. When you land, you'll pretend that you hurt your ankle.

You swing around one more time. Then you release your grip. You're sailing through the air . . .

Whoops! You flew a little too far. Right into the ring of fire that surrounds the landing mat.

Bad news. *Really* bad news.

You're not top dog.

You're a hot dog!

THE END

You fall about ten feet, then thud down beside Kim at the bottom of a pit. "Ow," you groan, climbing to your feet.

"Where are we?" Kim's voice shakes with terror.

"How should I know?" you snap.

You peer up at the opening of the pit. Too deep to climb out. But a dark tunnel yawns in front of you.

You have no choice. You have to walk through it.

You step cautiously forward. The air is thick and damp. You wonder if you're having a nightmare. If so, you can't wait to wake up!

The deeper you go, the darker the tunnel gets.

"It's so stuffy in here," complains Kim. "I can't breathe!"

She can't breathe? Hmm ... not a bad thing. Maybe that means she'll shut up! you think hopefully.

A moment later you step into a large cavern full of flasks and beakers. It looks like some sort of science lab.

Dim light fills the room, but you can't tell where it's coming from. At the far end, a cage hangs from the ceiling. You step closer. What's in there?

When you see, you clap a hand over your mouth to keep from screaming.

Go on to PAGE 127.

Can you swim to shore? It seems to be your only chance.

"Jump!" you shout to Kim.

The boat is only a few feet from the falls. The rushing water sounds like thunder.

You jump —

And choke, as a huge wave slaps you in the face. Swirling water grabs you and pulls you down, down . . . down to the bottom of the river. It tumbles you around and around, like laundry in a washing machine.

And it's pushing you toward the falls!

Your lungs are bursting. In another moment, they will fill with water. Your body is scraped and bruised from the rocks.

Why did you think you could swim away from a waterfall?

News flash:

You're all washed up!

THE END

You and Kim dash up to the mouth of the cave. The pack of hungry zombies is closing in on you.

"We're trapped!" Kim screams.

"Not yet!" you pant. You put your back against the big boulder and begin to shove as hard as you can.

"What are you doing?" Kim demands.

"Help me!" you cry. "We can start an avalanche!"

"It will never work," Kim declares. "Don't you know anything? Zombies are the living dead! You can't hurt them."

"Maybe not," you mutter. "But we can slow them down!"

You push harder on the rock. It starts to totter. And then it topples!

When the boulder hits the ground, part of the cliff collapses. A ton of rocks pours down the trail.

"UURRGHH!" the zombies moan as they're pelted with stones. Arms and legs fly in every direction. Heads roll.

The zombies haven't been destroyed. But it will be a long time before they can pull themselves together.

When the rocks stop falling, you step up to the opening to Zombie Cave. A faint light glows from inside.

Go to PAGE 126.

"I'll try the hike," you decide.

"Okay. Meet Coach Krump at the equipment shed," Coach Rex orders. He points out the shed to you. "Get going, camper!"

Four other kids are already waiting at the equipment shed when you get there. A dark-haired girl with braces smiles at you. "I'm Tracy," she says. "I'm going on the hike too."

The other kids introduce themselves as Samantha, Al, and Ted.

Samantha, a tall, strong-looking girl, beckons all four of you closer. "I've heard some strange things about this hike," she whispers. "They say some kids don't come back from it."

"Then why are you going?" Al asks.

"I want to win the Outdoors Medal," Samantha replies calmly.

You smile to yourself. Camps always have silly scary stories. You know Samantha is only trying to psych out the competition. But you're a good hiker. You plan to win that medal yourself.

"Here comes another hiker!" Ted exclaims.

You glance up and see someone running toward the shed.

"Oh, no!" you groan.

What's wrong? Find out on PAGE 36.

You hold your stomach, groaning. "Ooohh, I'm sick. Where's the infirmary?"

Charlie points to a low, white building across from the cafeteria. "Hope you make it back."

Huh? Why wouldn't you make it back?

At the infirmary door, a voice behind you makes you really groan. "Got a problem, camper?" Coach Rex asks.

"I've got a bad stomachache," you reply, doubled over.

Coach Rex shakes his head in disgust. "I knew you couldn't cut it."

He pushes you through the door of the infirmary, locking it behind you.

"Nurse, have you repaired the transporter yet?" he demands.

Transporter?

Turn to PAGE 33.

You pull yourself frantically up. Your arms ache.

You glance down. The zombie is trying to climb the cliff too. But it's clumsy. Its rotting fingers can't grasp the rocks.

Finally, it seems to give up. You hang there, halfway up the cliff, and watch as it vanishes into the trees.

Whew! "I think it's gone," you tell Kim. "Come on, let's head back down the cliff."

You've almost reached the bottom when you hear a growl.

Crouched in your path is a mountain lion!

The big cat's yellow eyes gaze hungrily at you. Uh-oh! "Head back up," you whisper.

But just as you inch up the cliff, a huge boulder bounds down the slope, just missing you.

"The zombie!" Kim cries. "It must have climbed up the trail! It's up at the top of the cliff!"

You duck as another boulder hurtles past your ear.

"Let's get out of here!" Kim cries.

Great idea, you think. But where to? If you head down, the mountain lion will attack.

And if you climb up, you'll have to face the zombie!

If you go down toward the mountain lion, turn to PAGE 101.

If you head up toward the zombie, turn to PAGE 54.

You cycle down a dirt road until you reach the highway.

You remember the old man down the road. You take a left to his house.

You jump off your bike and race up to the porch. *BRRING! BRRING!* You hit the doorbell again and again. Finally the old man opens the door. He's holding a pair of headphones.

"You're never going to believe this," you pant, "but Camp Running Leaf is sending kids to an alien planet as slaves!"

To your shock, the old man doesn't call the nearest mental hospital. Instead, he invites you in!

"I'm Agent Driscoll," he tells you. "I head up a government team that investigates alien activity."

You stare at him. This is incredible!

"We've had our suspicions about that camp for some time now. One of my field agents went to check it out," the old man goes on. "But she never made it back."

You remember the skull you saw in the lake. Shuddering, you pull out the ID card you found and show it to Agent Driscoll.

He nods sadly. "Draper was a good agent," he tells you. Then he brightens. "But at least now we've got enough evidence to get a search warrant!"

Join the search on PAGE 96.

SPLOOOSH!

The pipe empties you into a river. You gasp and splash, trying to keep your head above water.

After a few minutes, you manage to swim to shore. You climb an embankment and scramble onto a bridge by some railroad tracks.

A train whistle blows. You move off the tracks and wait. A minute later, a freight train rumbles by.

The train is moving slowly. You grab on to a ladder and haul yourself into an empty boxcar. You lean against a wall, dazed.

The rocking of the car lulls you. Your eyes feel heavy. Your chin falls to your chest.

The sound of someone clearing his throat wakes you up.

When you open your eyes —

Oh, no.

A tall, stern police officer is standing over you. Scowling.

Get arrested on PAGE 110.

"A snake!" Kim cries.

You look. "It's just a garter snake," you grumble. "Chill!"

A few minutes later, Kim screams again.

What now?

"Across the river!" she shrieks. "A z-z-zombie!"

You roll your eyes. "There's no such thing as zombies," you mutter. "Will you hurry? The other teams are going to beat us to Zombie Cave."

You slog down the trail. Kim sulks behind you.

Then she screams again. "The zombie! It's back! Look!"

"Oh, please," you grumble. You peer across the river.

Hey. What's that moving over there? Something tall and pale flickers between the trees.

"See?" Kim hisses in your ear.

"It's probably just another hiker," you say.

But suddenly you're not so sure.

You know zombies don't exist. But you wish Coach Krump hadn't talked so much about them.

You look again. Whatever it was, it's not there anymore.

Just another hiker, you tell yourself. Relax.

"Oh, no!" Kim cries. "Now we're *really* in trouble!"

Find the trouble on PAGE 46.

You turn left and race down the road. You keep running and running. Your legs burn, and your lungs feel as if they're about to burst.

Where is the old man's house? Was it some kind of mirage?

Suddenly a black shape looms out of the darkness.

There it is! The old man's house!

No lights are on. You approach the front door slowly.

Raising your fist, you knock. The door swings open. You peer into the dimly lit hall to see who answered it.

There's no one there!

You gulp. Should you go into this creepy place?

But then you hear the faint *TROMP! TROMP!* of many feet.

The campers! They're on your trail!

Looks as if you've run out of choices.

Check out the old man's house on PAGE 44.

"Come on!" you say to Kim. "Let's fight our way out!"

You take a swing at the nearest zombie.

SQUELCH! Your fist goes *into* its stomach!

Up to the elbow!

Big, BIG yuck!

The zombie falls back with a hideous moan. You feel like puking. But you don't have time right now. You and Kim dash up the trail leading to Zombie Cave.

You glance over your shoulder. The zombies stalk after you. They move slowly — but steadily.

And they look hungrier than ever!

"Head for the cave!" Kim shouts. "We'll be safe there!"

"In a place called *Zombie* Cave?" you reply. "I doubt it!"

But, peering around, you realize you have no choice. The cliff in front of you looks too sheer to climb.

The trail to the cave is steep and rocky. Very rocky. One especially big boulder balances on a ledge by the cave mouth.

Hmm. That gives you an idea.

Move on to PAGE 77!

You sail through the air. Your legs pump frantically, as if you're still running on ground. And then . . .

Your feet touch the track.

You made it!

Terror carries you down the track faster than you've ever run before. You whip along like a greyhound. You're going to win this race!

Suddenly, you hear a scream behind you.

You glance over your shoulder. It's Brad!

He has fallen — and he can't get up. He's lying at the edge of the snake pit. A diamondback rattler is coiled by his face — ready to strike!

"Help!" he cries. "If I move, it will bite me!"

You've had enough of Brad and his tricks. Let him help himself, you think.

Then you think again. Brad may be a jerk — but he's a jerk in need.

Maybe you should go back and help him.

If you help Brad, go to PAGE 41.
If you don't help Brad, go to PAGE 5.

You can't believe who is standing behind you.

"Uncle Ed!" you cry.

"At last!" Uncle Ed says. He's carrying a flashlight. By its glow, you can see that he looks tired and worried. "I've been searching for you for hours!"

"Am I glad to see you!" you exclaim. The whole incredible story pours out of you. About the zombies. And Coach Krump.

"I'm sorry," Uncle Ed says when you've finished talking. "I never should have brought you on this mission."

"Mission?" You stare at your uncle in confusion.

Uncle Ed glances around to make sure no one is listening. "You see, I'm with the X-Factors," he whispers. "It's a secret security organization. We investigate unnatural events. On the way to Camp Pendleton, I made a phone call, remember?"

You nod, dazed. The *X-Factors*?

"That was when I got the assignment to investigate Camp Running Leaf. There were rumors the Cemetery Man was there."

"The Cemetery Man?" you exclaim. "But Coach Krump said there was no such person as the Cemetery Man."

Uncle Ed shakes his head. "He was lying," he tells you. "Coach Krump *is* the Cemetery Man!"

Learn the whole, horrible truth on PAGE 49.

You strain your ears to hear more.

"I heard one of the specimens gave you some trouble this morning," the other coach says. "Started a food fight."

"Yeah," Coach Rex growls. "Kid wouldn't eat the eggs. But the rest are chowing down on them three times a day. Getting stronger and more obedient."

"They'd better be. Or the masters on Xentron will rearrange our organs."

"Ouch!" Coach Rex exclaims. "I hate when that happens!"

Are you dreaming this? You pinch yourself.

Yeow! That hurt!

You start to panic. Because this *definitely* is no dream.

Turn to PAGE 68.

You doze off. The sound of a car honking wakes you up.

Cautiously, you peer around the corner of the gas station.

"Uncle Ed!" you cry when you recognize his car. You run to the station wagon.

You yank open the passenger door — only to find that it's already occupied.

By Coach Rex!

The coach grabs your wrist. "No more escapes for you," he snarls as he loads you into the backseat.

"Uncle Ed, what's happening?" you plead.

"I took you to Camp Running Leaf instead of Camp Pendleton on purpose," he says. "Our alien masters pay me well to direct kids here. It's a recruiting station for Xentronian mine slaves."

"But — but you're my own uncle!" you wail.

Uncle Ed shrugs. "Sorry about that. Just business. Nothing personal. Now, where can I drop you off, Rex?"

"The infirmary," Rex commands. "From there, this camper is going on a long trip."

"Right." Uncle Ed chuckles and turns to you. "Well, kid, soon you'll be shoveling klatu crystals in a Xentronian mine. I hope you dig the experience!"

THE END

"Gotcha!" cries a familiar voice.

"Kim!" you scream.

You whirl around angrily. Kim is standing behind you with a stupid grin on her face.

"What did you think, I was a zombie?" Kim asks. She laughs.

"Funny!" you grumble.

"Don't you know there's no such thing as zombies?" Kim adds.

"I know that," you snap. "I knew it was you. I was looking for you. My map is wrong. I wanted to compare it with yours."

"You never could follow a map," Kim declares. "So I guess you have to follow *me*." She giggles. "That is, if you're not too scared to hike with me."

You swallow an angry comment. Payback will come later.

Meanwhile, you want that Outdoors Medal. And you've already wasted a couple of hours.

It looks as if you have no choice.

Turn to PAGE 118.

The bugle sounds for dinner, but you ignore it. You have a pretty good idea what they're serving.

Instead, you lie on your bunk, thinking.

Why are the eggs blue?

And why is it so important that the campers eat them?

Pat returns from dinner. "You missed great eggs Benedict," he drones. "You should eat them like everyone else."

Your stomach growls. "I wasn't hungry," you lie.

A few other campers straggle into the cabin. You introduce yourself. They barely look at you.

To break the ice, you say, "Coach Rex acts like this is a boot camp, not a sports camp."

A kid named Preston stares at you. "Don't put down our master coach. He should be respected and obeyed."

Pat adds, "Don't make waves. Just get with the program."

Man! They sound like robots!

The bugle sounds again. This time it's playing taps. Lights go out all over the camp. No one laughs or tells stories.

You feel very alone in this creepy camp.

Go on to PAGE 42.

You reach into your pack and grab the survival kit. You open it with shaking fingers.

Your heart falls right down to your toes.

All the kit contains is a bar of soap and a sewing kit!

Wait a second.

A sewing kit?

Maybe that's the answer!

Check out the plan on PAGE 117.

Slowly, carefully, you sneak off down the track. All eyes are on Brad. No one sees you go.

You dash to the cafeteria. All right! The mountain bike still gleams in the glass case.

You break the case, wheel the bike outside, and climb on.

And you're off!

With everyone's attention focused on Brad, the coaches don't realize what you've done — until you're halfway across the field. You throw the bike into the highest gear and stand up to pedal.

Hey. This is your best event yet!

You zoom past the gatehouse at the other end of the camp. Rex and the other coaches give chase. But they're on foot. You're on wheels. They can't catch you!

You're escaping from Camp Run-for-Your-Life!

Pedal to PAGE 81.

You check to make sure no one is looking. Then you casually put your napkin on top of your eggs, fold them inside, and slip it under the table.

A second later, you hear a voice behind you. "I saw that!"

You freeze. It's Coach Rex.

Rex points at another camper and barks, "You spit out your eggs. Don't let it happen again."

The camper, a tough-looking kid with a black buzz-cut, nods.

You let out a sigh of relief as Rex walks away. He didn't see you hide the eggs.

"Who's the guy who didn't eat the eggs?" you ask Pat.

"His name's Brad," Pat answers.

Doo-doo doot-a-doot, doo-doo doot-a-doot! A bugle blows reveille outside. The campers rise as one and march to the door in neat files. No one talks. No horseplay.

"You know what I call Camp Running Leaf?" Pat whispers to you. "Camp Run-for-Your-Life."

You grin at his joke.

Pat doesn't smile back.

Go on to PAGE 106.

"I want to do the hurdles," you tell Pat.

"Me too," he agrees. "I hate swimming."

You follow Coach Rex to the track. You and Pat line up with the other kids. Coach Rex points a starter's pistol in the air. "Runners on your mark!"

You step into the starting blocks.

"Get set!" Coach Rex calls.

You set your hands in the dirt. Then you glance up to check out the hurdles.

You can't believe your eyes.

The first hurdle is higher than your waist. Its two legs are tipped with gleaming swords. And the crossbar is a wicked-looking rusty saw! If you land on that, you've had it!

Pat gulps. "Oh, no!"

BANG!

The runners take off.

You and Pat take off too. But in the *other* direction.

You're not about to jump over those deadly hurdles!

"Come back here!" Coach Rex roars.

You spy a small door near the edge of the stadium.

"Come on!" you cry to Pat. "Let's get out of here!"

Turn to PAGE 112.

Agent Driscoll immediately gets on the phone to Washington.

The problem is, it takes a long time to get a search warrant. By the time the authorities finally arrive at Camp Running Leaf, the grounds are deserted. The coaches, campers, and transporter are gone. There isn't even a scrap of blue egg.

However, Agent Driscoll doesn't lose heart. "I'm certain Coach Rex and the Xentronians will soon start up another camp for human slaves," he tells you as he drives you home.

Another Camp Run-for-Your-Life.

It could be anywhere in the country.

It could even be the next camp *you* go to!

THE END

"It's the kitchen!" Pat whispers.

Workers scurry in and out through the swinging doors in the far wall. Two cooks in aprons bustle back and forth among bubbling vats and giant grills.

"That stuff in the vat! It's blue, just like the eggs," you point out.

The blue liquid is poured over some freshly broken eggs. The cooks fry them on the grill.

One of the cooks stops to fan himself. He glances around, as if he's making sure no one is looking. Then he picks up a spray bottle and sprays himself.

Huh? His face! It's . . . melting!

No, you realize. What you thought was his face is actually a thick layer of stage makeup.

But that's nothing compared to what you see underneath.

His skin is tinted blue.

His eyes are golden.

He has no nose.

There's a small round hole in the top of his head.

"He's . . . he's not human!" Pat gasps.

Save your gasps until PAGE 115.

Enough worrying about Pat. You decide to check out the soccer game.

When you reach the field, one of the goalies is holding a hand over his swollen, purple nose. It looks broken to you.

"Go to the nurse, Antoine!" his teammates yell at him. "You can't play anymore."

"I don't want to leave my goal area!" Antoine cries in a plugged-up voice. "And I'm not going to the nurse. No one comes back from the infirmary!"

Your eyes widen. Is Antoine serious?

A tall girl grabs you. "You can play goalie, can't you?"

What should you do? You could replace Antoine as the goalie, or you could volunteer to play forward instead.

If you agree to play goalie, turn to PAGE 20.
If you'd rather play forward, turn to PAGE 53.

It's a good thing you played goalie and saved your energy. Because now you're able to stay awake.

Rex and the other coach finally move on.

You quietly dress and creep out of the cabin. Your plan is to find a phone and call Uncle Ed for help. But after a few minutes of searching, you realize the truth.

There are no phones at Camp Running Leaf.

Well, it makes sense — in a horrifying way. They don't want anyone to contact the outside world.

Then, in the distance, you hear Coach Rex's voice on the loudspeaker. "Alert! Alert! Escaped camper!"

You listen more closely. Now you hear what sounds like a hundred people marching together. *TROMP. TROMP. TROMP.*

The marching feet are coming your way!

Oh, no! If they catch you, you're in major trouble!

Go on to PAGE 19.

100

"What's this?" a voice booms. "Two athletes not competing?"

You groan. You know that voice.

Coach Rex!

Coach Rex waves some workers over. "Maybe they haven't eaten enough eggs. They need a direct transfusion. Hold them down."

Your arms are pinned. A moment later, the blue-skinned alien is standing over you. The plastic tube is in his head again. He places the other end in your left ear.

NO!

You stare in helpless horror as the fluid begins to flow. . . .

Down the tube.

Into your ear.

"Your brain is being bathed in our special fluid," Coach Rex informs you. "It will make you completely obedient."

As the last shreds of your own free will leave you, you think, I guess this is what they mean by *brainwashing*. . . .

THE END

You'd much rather face a mountain lion than a walking corpse, you think.

You glance at the mountain lion again. It kind of reminds you of your cat, Smokey, back home.

"We can handle the cat!" you tell Kim confidently. You pace toward the beast. "Here, kitty, kitty," you croon.

Kim stays a couple of steps behind you.

The mountain lion's yellow eyes don't blink. It crouches there, its tail twitching. You're starting to wonder if this was such a good idea. The beast still reminds you of Smokey ... when she's getting ready to kill a mouse!

You gulp. Maybe you should back up.

Too late. Before you've gone three steps, the big cat springs!

What happens next?

Well, we'd really rather not go into details.

But we'd be lion if we said it wasn't ...

THE END.

You can't let Kim face a flesh-eating zombie alone. You turn back and grab her hands.

"Come on!" you cry, pulling her up. "We'll lose the zombie in the woods."

Kim leans on you. The two of you stumble into the trees. You hear the zombie crashing through the trees.

"FOOOO!" it moans. "UURRGGHH!"

Quickly, you switch directions.

And then — the woods are silent.

Where did the zombie go? Did you lose it?

Or is it laying some kind of trap for you?

You sniff the air. Is it your imagination? Or can you catch a faint whiff of rotting flesh?

"Hurry," you urge Kim. You drag her along.

The rotten smell grows stronger.

And then you crash right into a tall, dark form.

Turn to PAGE 48.

Without thinking, you grab the alligator's jaws. *SNAP!* You shut them. It's as easy as closing a suitcase.

The alligator glares at you.

CREEEEAKK! It forces its jaws open again.

SNAP! You glare back and shut them again.

CREEEAAK! It opens them back up.

SNAP!

CREEEAAKK!

SN ——

CREEEEAAKK!

CHOMP!

GULP!

BUUUURPPPP!

THE END

A huge hand grabs you.

"Who are you?" barks the huge guy attached to the huge hand.

"Uh, I-I'm from Camp Running Leaf," you reply meekly.

A woman comes up. "I'm Agent Alice Draper. We're with the government. We've been monitoring transmissions from a planet eight light-years from Earth. The transmissions have been traced to Camp Running Leaf." She raises an eyebrow at you. "What can you tell us about the camp, kid?"

You repeat what you heard Coach Rex say about Xentron.

Draper's eyes light up. "This is amazing. The camp must hold incredibly advanced technology. Good job, camper."

The next few days are a blur. The government sweeps in by helicopter and raids the camp. Coach Rex and the rest of the staff are arrested for kidnapping, conducting business with an alien government without a license, and — worst of all — not paying their taxes.

The arrests so anger the Xentronians, they invade Earth.

Way to go. You're responsible for the total destruction of the human race!

Oops!

THE END

You sure did a lot of running around when you played forward. Now you're exhausted.

Try as you might, you can't keep your eyes open. Coach Rex's voice becomes a gentle buzz. . . .

You dream that Pat is forcing blue eggs down your throat. You struggle, choking. But you can't stop him.

The sound of the loudspeaker blaring reveille jolts you awake. It's morning. Automatically, you get out of bed.

That's when you glance down at the T-shirt you slept in.

It's smeared with blue eggs!

Pat is standing in the doorway with a wicked grin. "You're one of us now."

You feel different. Mellow, obedient. You wish only to do as you're told.

And later, when the blue-skinned Xentronian overlords tell you to dig for klatu crystals, you ask only one question: How deep, sir?

THE END

Outside, Coach Rex announces, "Fun time is over."

He stares at the campers. "You've eaten your eggs. You should be ready. The Selection is about to begin. And remember: The winner gets a very special prize!"

Rex checks his watch. "All athletes who think they are worthy of it, report to the stadium right now!"

"You're not going to do it, are you?" Pat whispers.

"Of course I am," you reply. You practically drool, thinking of the new mountain bike gleaming in the cafeteria.

Coach Rex claps his hands. "Let's go!"

You join the eerily silent stream of campers heading for the stadium. The other campers may be stronger. But you want that bike more than they do!

The coaches are waiting for you at one end of the field.

"Listen up, people," Coach Rex bellows. "The Selection runs like this: The athlete with the most points at the end gets the special prize. For the first event, you can choose between hurdles and swimming."

What are you good at? Do you want to jump hurdles? Or would you rather go swimming?

If you choose hurdles, turn to PAGE 95.
If you choose swimming, turn to PAGE 63.

You do a quick frog kick to get to the surface and escape the alligator.

The frog kick? Are you serious?

Alligators love frogs — especially for lunch! Now the big reptile *really* wants to eat you!

You make it to the surface, where you scramble atop a floating log. You hope you can escape the alligator up there.

As if.

The moment you turn around, you're facing a pair of wide-open jaws. And the jaws are about to chomp down on you!

What now?

Turn to PAGE 103.

108

You grab the crowbar.

The alligator's mouth gapes wide to chomp on you. You thrust the crowbar inside its choppers.

The crowbar wedges the huge alligator's jaws open.

That gives you the chance to swim away!

You pop to the surface and swim as hard as you can.

You're the last one to the finish line. As you lie gasping on the shore, Brad gloats: "Did you swim here — or take a rowboat? By the way, I came in first!"

"There was an alligator —" you gasp. You can hardly talk. Your teeth are chattering from fright.

Your comment catches Coach Karla's ear. "Alligator? Did you say you fought off an alligator?"

"Yes! And it's right over there!" you scream.

Turn to PAGE 22.

You stare at the map again. This is crazy! you tell yourself. You turn the map around.

It's no better upside down.

Maybe the problem is you. You're not that good with maps.

You think back to your geography project with Kim. She was a pain — but she was good at reading maps. Maybe you should have teamed up with her after all!

Maybe it's not too late. If you can find Kim, the two of you might be able to figure out how to find Zombie Cave.

The only problem is, where is Kim? She's probably on the main trail, you guess.

But which way *is* the main trail?

You're going to need a map of your own — and some good luck — to bring you back to the main trail. Here's what you do:

Find a map of the United States. Locate the Mississippi River on the map. Then, with your eyes closed, circle your finger around and let it land on the map.

If your finger lands west of the Mississippi (that's left!), turn left on PAGE 61.

If your finger lands east of the Mississippi (that's right!), go right on PAGE 121.

110

You try to explain about Camp Run-for-Your-Life. But the cop takes you to the station house, anyway.

A bearded man is talking to the desk sergeant. "Hey, Ruthie," the cop who arrested you calls. "You've got to hear this kid's story! Go on, kid, tell the desk sergeant."

So you tell your story to the desk sergeant. You notice that the bearded man is listening closely.

When you're done, the desk sergeant rolls her eyes. "This kid is nuts," she declares.

"Are you kidding?" the guy with the beard sputters. "That's the best story I've ever heard." He jumps up and approaches you. "Kid, my name is Vincent Vealberg. I make movies. And I'd like to buy your story."

A few months later the movie version of *Escape from Camp Run-for-Your-Life* hits the screens. It's the biggest hit in history. You become the richest kid in America.

You decide to use the money to start your own camp. You've even got the perfect name for it:

Camp Run-to-the-Bank!

THE END

Half hidden behind a bush is a wooden sign. You brush the leaves out of the way to read: CAMP AHEAD.

You're back at Camp Running Leaf!

You didn't much like the camp. But you can't wait to get back now! You follow the sign up a small hill, then gaze down.

In the valley below is a huge camp. A big sign in the front says WELCOME TO CAMP PENDLETON!

Camp Pendleton? Have you made a mistake?

No! you realize. Camp Pendleton was the camp you were supposed to attend in the first place! It was the camp Uncle Ed promised to take you to. Going to Camp Running Leaf was a mistake — a big mistake!

You rush down the hill to Camp Pendleton. Forget about Running Leaf, the Outdoors Medal, Kim, and the zombies.

You just hope you're not too late for breakfast!

THE END

112

You and Pat dash through the little door and slam it behind you.

"Something's really wrong with this camp," you pant.

"No kidding," Pat shoots back. "The blue eggs. The brainwashed campers. The crazy events they make us do. It's all very suspicious."

You peer around. You're at the mouth of a dark, tunnel-like hall. It slopes downhill. It's lined with huge pipes.

"I bet this is an old heating system for the camp," Pat says. "If we keep going, maybe it'll connect to another building."

"Then let's book," you say impatiently.

You move cautiously through the darkness. You pass an opening on the left. You think about exploring it, but then you notice the moldy smell seeping out.

You'll pass, you think.

Finally the tunnel ends — at a metal door. Light comes through a small window set high in the door. On tiptoes, you and Pat peer through the window.

See what you see on PAGE 97.

You and Kim toil up the mountain. It takes all afternoon. But the most tiring part of the hike isn't the climbing.

It's listening to Kim complain!

At last you spot what you came for. In the face of a cliff is a dark, forbidding hole. Zombie Cave! A trail leads down to it from where you are.

You and Kim hike down the steep trail. About halfway down, you hear a strange noise. A combination cough and growl.

"What's that?" Kim asks nervously.

"Zombies!" you reply in a spooky voice.

Kim shrieks.

"Just kidding," you tell her grinning.

As you continue down, you hear the sound again.

Hmm. It seems to be following you.

"Ignore it," you tell Kim. You're almost at the cave mouth.

You run ahead of Kim and enter the cave alone.

But when you see what is waiting inside, you freeze.

Go on to PAGE 18.

114

"I'll be the zombie," you volunteer.

Uncle Ed nods. "I'm counting on you," he tells you.

You and Uncle Ed follow the zombies' trail through the dark woods. It is almost dawn before you catch up with the hideous creatures. They're on a ridge overlooking Camp Running Leaf.

You peer out from behind a tree trunk. The zombie kids are sitting around a small campfire. If their eyes weren't open, you'd swear they were all dead.

They *are* dead, you remind yourself.

Coach Krump is pacing back and forth. He drones, "First we will take over Camp Running Leaf. Next we'll conquer . . ." It sounds like he's addressing the troops! you think with disgust.

Uncle Ed taps you on the shoulder. "Go," he mouths.

You swallow hard. Here goes nothing, you say to yourself. You step into the flickering light of the campfire.

Step over to PAGE 12.

You can't believe it. You don't know whether the kitchen worker is a space alien or some kind of weird mutant.

All you know is, you're having a close encounter of the weird kind!

"Whoa. I'm outta here!" you sputter.

Pat stops you. "There's nowhere to go. Let's wait until the cooks take a break. Then we'll slip out through the kitchen. I bet those swinging doors lead outside."

You're about to okay his plan. But then you remember: Wasn't there a turnoff in the tunnel?

Should you wait until the coast is clear in the kitchen? Or should you go back down the tunnel and take the turnoff?

If you wait to go out through the kitchen, turn to PAGE 23.

If you go back down the tunnel, turn to PAGE 13.

116

You swim closer. You're terrified. But you have to get a closer look at the skull.

A crowbar lies next to it. And there's something square and white a couple of feet away. It looks like an ID card or something.

You've got to go up for air. Grabbing the white square, you bring it to the surface. It's a plastic ID card. You can just make out the words U.S. GOVERNMENT through the muck.

This is serious. The ID badge of a government agent at the bottom of the lake — next to a human skull!

How did the skull and the badge get there?

And why is there a crowbar next to them?

You have to go back for another look.

You suck in a big breath and dive to the bottom.

As you approach the skull, you notice something odd. Two small yellow lights. Moving toward you.

You swim to the skull. The lights are still coming.

Two black dots appear in the centers of the yellow lights.

Your blood suddenly goes cold.

Those aren't lights. They're EYES!

Get a closer look on PAGE 55.

Quickly, you thread the needle. You snatch up the zombie's arm from the ground.

"What are you doing?" Kim shrieks.

"Just watch," you say tensely. You hold the arm out.

"Hey, zombie," you call as calmly as you can.

The armless zombie gazes at you suspiciously.

You stick the needle into the arm. Then you pull the thread all the way through.

"Ecch!" Kim exclaims.

You press the arm against the zombie's shoulder. Then you push the needle in. It moves easily through the soft, rotten flesh. You swallow hard and try not to hurl.

A few quick stitches, and the arm is attached again.

The zombie stares at you. Then it opens its mouth in a big, drooling smile. "Oooo!" it crows. "Uuuuurrrrghhh!"

The other zombies crowd around, touching the stitches. "Uuurgh!" they murmur. Their voices sound excited.

Your plan worked! The zombies are no longer angry.

But now you have another problem.

Face it on PAGE 6.

118

You sigh. "All right, let's team up," you say to Kim.

You watch while she studies her map. You hate to admit it, but it's true: Kim is a much better map-reader than you.

"Zombie Cave is on the other side of Zombie Mountain," she remarks, pointing to a squiggle on the map. "Also, the campsite is on the same side of the mountain as the cave," she continues. "They look close to each other."

"So let's get started," you say impatiently.

"Wait," Kim cautions. "According to the map, there are two ways to get to the cave. We could take the main trail up over the mountain. But it's very steep."

"What's the other way?" you ask.

"The other way is to follow the river around the mountain," she explains. "But it's much longer. Also" — she squints at the paper — "there are some strange markings I can't figure out."

You glance at her map. "X's" line the riverbank.

"You decide. Which route seems easiest?" Kim asks you.

You study the map. Both routes look tough to you.

Which one will you take?

If you climb the mountain, start on PAGE 113.
If you follow the river, begin on PAGE 16.

Coach Rex leads you to the track. "The last event is called the steeplechase," he announces.

You've seen that event on TV. It's the one where you run 3,000 meters around the track. But there are obstacles, like high hurdles and pools of water. You can push off the top of the heavy hurdle to vault over the water.

The event looks harmless. No flames. No one throwing spears at you.

Then Coach Rex smiles. "Whoever survives this race deserves the prize," he declares.

The word "survive" makes you gulp.

You glance up nervously at the stands.

There are exactly seven campers left.

And they're moving toward the infirmary.

Turn to PAGE 57.

The smell comes from the lake you're about to swim in!

Coach Karla announces, "Swimmers line up! The 400-meter swamp swim will begin in thirty seconds. The longer you wait, the hungrier the alligators get!"

Alligators? Your heart thumps. Brad looks worried too.

But none of the other campers seem troubled. They just do what they're told. They must know Coach Karla is a kidder, you think.

You gaze down at the murky brown water. Bubbles come up from under the surface. Big bubbles.

"Swimmers, on your mark . . ."

For a moment you think about skipping this event.

Then you remember the gleaming new mountain bike.

You bend your knees and thrust your arms back.

"Get set . . ."

BANG!

Dive in on PAGE 124.

You decide to take the right-hand fork.

You take a gulp of water, then start toward the right. The trees are thick on this trail. The farther you go, the harder it is to move. Branches and twigs scrape your face and arms.

You stop to catch your breath.

And you hear something behind you.

Something large.

THUMP, THUMP, THUMP go its heavy steps.

Maybe it's only my imagination, you think hopefully.

But the thumping noise gets closer. And now you hear something else.

Breathing. Hoarse, raspy breathing.

You break into a run, scrambling through the trees. You stumble blindly, trying to escape from whatever is behind you.

And then —

Something grabs you around the neck.

Go on to PAGE 90.

122

"Wait for a better chance," you quickly tell Brad.

You square your shoulders. Then you run toward the bar.

Flames lick at your feet as you swing up. But you ignore them and concentrate on your routine.

Good thing you took gymnastics last summer at your other camp. You're good at this stuff!

Every flip and spin could land you in the fire. But you've never worked the bar so well — even though your shorts are starting to smell scorched.

Uh-oh. The hot bar is starting to blister your palms. Better finish up your routine now. Otherwise you won't just get a low mark. You'll get third-degree burns!

You swing into your dismount. A glance at the mat tells you you have to make a perfect landing. One step in the wrong direction and you'll be in the fire.

Can you do it? Can you stick your landing?

Turn to PAGE 65.

"I'm in," you reply instantly. "But how can we stop the Cemetery Man?"

"The first thing is, we've got to get the zombie-making chemical from him," Uncle Ed replies. "As I mentioned, the side effect on humans is temporary. If they don't get a fresh dose of the chemical every day for a month, the effect will wear off."

It will wear off? What a relief!

That means there's hope for the other hikers.

Even Kim!

Uncle Ed continues. "Here's the plan. One of us will pretend to be a zombie. The pretend-zombie will distract Krump. Then the other will take the water gun from him."

"Uh — okay," you say doubtfully.

To tell the truth, the plan sounds kind of lame to you.

But you don't have any better ideas.

The next question is: Who gets to play the zombie?

If you want to act as a zombie, turn to PAGE 114.

If you want to go for the water gun, turn to PAGE 45.

124

You hit the water hard. Then you take a few strokes underwater.

You come up gasping for air. The water is thick with mud and vegetation. It feels as though you landed in a bowl of pudding.

You swim hard, trying to block out the putrid smell.

Sputtering and gasping for air, you lift your head. Brad is ahead. You plow on, trying to catch him.

Then you hear a cry. You see a pair of arms grasping for help above the water.

And then — they disappear under the water!

Oh, no! One of the other kids is in trouble!

What are you going to do? Dive into the muck to save the kid who went under?

Or should you get help from Coach Karla?

If you dive down, turn to PAGE 37.
If you swim back to Coach Karla for help, turn to PAGE 11.

"I'll do the Selection," you tell Coach Rex.

Coach Rex smiles. "Good. Maybe you'll go far after all. And I mean *far*." He starts chuckling, as if he's made a big joke.

You laugh politely.

Now the coach gets serious. "The Selection is tough. If you're going to win," he says, "you need strength. And that means a big breakfast. Come on down to the chow hall."

The coach takes you to a big cafeteria, where the other kids are eating breakfast.

Everyone stares at you when you walk in. Then they go back to their breakfasts. Each kid has a big pile of eggs. They quietly scarf down their food. No one's talking much.

You notice a mountain bike in a glass case on the wall. It's top of the line. And it's brand-new. Sunlight gleams on its blue carbon-fiber frame.

That must be the special prize for winning the Selection, you think.

Cool! Now you *really* want to win!

Go on to PAGE 40.

Carefully, you and Kim poke your heads into Zombie Cave.

"Hello?" you call, hoping no one will answer.

Whew! No one does. The cave is empty!

You peer down at the floor. No footprints in the loose soil. You must be the first hikers to reach the cave.

"Come on!" Kim says impatiently. "Let's find the bones."

Where is the light coming from? you wonder. Then you notice faint green streaks of glowing minerals in the cave walls.

A quick search doesn't turn up any bones.

First you feel disappointed.

Then you feel something on your leg. It tickles.

Absently you reach down to scratch your thigh.

Aaagh! A giant spider crawls onto your hand!

With a yell, you flick the spider away. It flies off your hand and lands on a glittering object, half buried in the cave floor.

A gold ring!

"Maybe we should dig here," you suggest eagerly. "We might find buried treasure!"

Or you might find buried terror.

See what's there on PAGE 71.

On first sight, the cage seems filled with humans.

On second sight, it seems filled with *ex*-humans.

They are dressed in rags and are partly decomposed. As if they were corpses. Except they're somehow alive. Like . . .

Zombies!

The creatures moan hideously. One of them shakes the bars of the cage with its rotting hands. It clacks its teeth at you. "Foo!" it cries in a groaning voice. "Foo fo fawt!"

What's that? Is the zombie trying to speak?

Kim jumps behind you, trying to use you as a shield. "Zombies!" she shrieks. "Let's get out of here — now!"

For once, you agree with her. Your knees tremble with fear. Turning, you stumble back toward the dark tunnel.

But then a tall, bulky figure steps out and blocks your way.

Turn to PAGE 59.

Your fingernails dig into the track. Terror adds to your strength. If you fall, you've had it!

With a mighty effort, you haul yourself out of the pit. You get to your feet. Your legs are wobbling.

Coach Rex smiles. "Good work. Now move it!"

You were always a good runner. It's time to pour it on. You increase your pace and pull even with Brad. Then you're ahead.

Not being stupid, you're pretty cautious about the next hurdle. You pull up short and peer over the jump. What's on the other side?

Whoa.

It's a pit full of writhing, twisting, hissing snakes!

You don't need a field guide to reptiles to recognize some of the most poisonous snakes in the world. Cobras. Rattlers. Pit vipers. Coral snakes.

"What are you waiting for?" Coach Rex shouts. "Do I have to come in there and *make* you jump?"

You glance back. He's striding toward you.

Holding one of the javelins from the javelin catch!

You have no choice. Taking a deep breath, you fling your body up into the air.

See if you made it on PAGE 86.

Suddenly the sound of the waterfall gets much more distant.

You open your eyes. The boat bobs in a quiet inlet.

Excellent! You made it into the little stream!

"I wonder where we are," you say, gazing around.

"I'm too seasick to read the map," Kim moans. She hands it to you.

You glance at the map. Even you can figure this one out. A trail from the shore goes a little way up the mountain. It dead-ends in a cliff. But you can see the dark hole in the cliff from where you are.

"There's Zombie Cave!" you exclaim. "Come on!"

Climbing over the side of the rowboat, you wade ashore. The water doesn't even come up to your knees.

Kim, of course, doesn't climb out. Not until you've dragged the boat up on the bank so she won't get her feet wet.

The two of you start up the trail to the cave.

You're almost there when a terrifying moan stops you.

You peer up the slope in the fading sunlight.

Yikes! A monster is staring down at you!

Go on to PAGE 134.

You turn around.

Coach Krump is standing there, water gun in hand.

Okay, so you're a zombie.

As it turns out, though, being a zombie is not the worst thing in the world. True, within a month, most of your skin rots away. Your teeth and hair fall out. You lose all of your toes.

But no one makes any cracks about it.

That's because, thanks to the Cemetery Man and his army, everyone else in the world has *also* been turned into a zombie.

And all you zombies live — uh, that is, *don't* live — happily ever after!

THE END

You unroll your sleeping bag. This is fine, you tell yourself. I'll just find the campsite in the morning.

If you're still alive in the morning.

You eat a candy bar. Then you snuggle into your sleeping bag. You'll have to stay awake all night. You don't dare fall asleep. If you do, zombies could sneak up on you.

You lie in the sleeping bag, staring at the moon.

But gradually, your eyes flutter closed. . . .

When you open them again, everything is pitch-dark.

You try to sit up. But something is wrapped around you. You can't see or hear! You scream like a maniac.

Then you realize:

You zipped yourself into your sleeping bag, dummy!

When you finally struggle out of the sleeping bag, sunlight floods your eyes. It's a beautiful morning.

But the woods are still full of zombies, you think. And Kim is out there by herself, where you left her.

You've got to go back for her!

When you reach the clearing, there's no sign of her.

But you notice something you missed last night.

Find it on PAGE 111.

You crack up. "There's no such thing as zombies," you snort.

"Are you sure?" Coach Krump narrows his eyes at you. "Why do you think they call it Zombie Mountain?"

You know he's just fooling. But he sounds awfully serious.

"Wh-what do zombies look like?" Kim asks.

"They're the walking dead," Coach Krump replies. "They crave living flesh. A zombie's bite will turn you into a zombie."

You and Al snicker.

"It's not funny," Coach Krump says solemnly. "Every year we lose a few campers to zombies."

Okay, the coach is just trying to make the hike more fun. But isn't he going a little overboard?

Ted pipes up, "I've heard stories about a strange guy who lives on Zombie Mountain. They call him the Cemetery Man."

Krump scowls. "He doesn't exist," he snaps. "Okay, people! The gear is in the shed. Take what you need and get started."

You take a sleeping bag, pack, food, and flashlight. Coach Krump hands you a map and a box labeled SURVIVAL KIT.

You're turning to go when the coach stops you. "Wait!" he exclaims. "I forgot to tell you the most important thing of all. No matter what, you *must* reach the campsite by midnight!"

Go on to PAGE 50.

"Wh-what do you mean?" you ask in a shaking voice.

"The Outdoors Medal," Coach Krump says. "All the others got theirs. Maybe I forgot to mention the rules before," he adds. "See, the only way to earn a medal — is to become a zombie!"

"No!" you howl. You try to crawl away.

But it's no use. The zombie kids grab you. Kim bites your arm. Al tears at your legs.

Seconds later, your heart stops. Your breathing stops. Your brain stops. Your entire body turns cold.

Coach Krump places a medal around your neck.

In camp, it glittered like gold. But actually, the medal is made of cheap plastic. There's a picture of a zombie etched in the center. Around the edge of the pendant are the words: KISS ME, I'M A ZOMBIE!

THE END

134

The creature stands directly in front of you. It is the size of an adult man. But it's missing an arm. Its other arm and its legs are covered with sores and scabs.

Its face is a thing from your nightmares. Half the skin has rotted off its skull. One eye is missing. Two black teeth dangle from its gums.

Kim screams, "It's a zombie!"

You gasp and start backing down the path.

"Foo!" the creature cries. It staggers after you.

You whirl and begin to run.

"Go!" you scream to Kim. "Run back to the boat!"

It's nearly dark. It's hard to see where you're going. You slip and slide on the rocky trail. At last you see the boat.

But there's another zombie on the path in front of it!

You skid to a stop just before you run into the hideous thing. You spin, looking for an escape route.

Too late. You and Kim are completely surrounded.

Surrounded by hideous, undead creatures!

Turn to PAGE 21 — if you dare!

You circle around until you're behind the zombies.

Then, from a safe distance, you follow the hideous band. It's easy to keep track of them in the dark. They smell like a garbage dump!

With luck, you'll be able to warn the other campers in time.

The zombies shuffle through the dark woods.

Suddenly Coach Krump calls a halt. "I hear something," he rasps. "Maybe it's that kid who got away."

Holding your breath, you duck behind a rock.

A mosquito bites you. Swatting at it, you slap your arm.

Oops! Did anyone hear that?

"Uuuuurrrrggghhh!" someone says right behind you.

Uh-oh.

You run as fast as you can — for about three feet.

Then you trip.

When you look up, you're surrounded by zombies. Their undead faces stare hungrily at you. As if you're junk food.

"Congratulations," Coach Krump tells you. "You've almost earned your medal."

Medal? Move on to PAGE 133.

The fastball is too tempting. You lace it to left for a single. You stand on first base, grinning.

But the first-base coach grabs you and throws you out of the game. "You were told to make a sacrifice bunt," he fumes. "You disobeyed an order."

As he pushes you off the field, the other players shake their heads.

"Obey the rules!" the first baseman calls in a dull voice.

"Follow orders!" your pal, Pat, sneers.

"Respect authority!" another kid chimes in.

"Aren't you guys taking the game a little too seriously?" you ask.

The coach turns to the others and says, "What do we do to those who aren't team players?"

The campers chant in one voice, "Sacrifice! Sacrifice!"

All the players stalk toward you with their bats raised. That's when you realize the horrible truth: They're not talking about a sacrifice *bunt*.

You got to first base.

Too bad you'll never make it home!

THE END

"Oooh, I don't like graveyards," Kim whines. "Why did we have to come this way?"

"Don't ask me. You're the one with the map!" you retort.

Then you notice something odd.

A glass beaker, the kind they use in science labs, is lying on top of a gravestone. You step closer, squinting at the white label on the beaker.

"'Property of the Cemetery Man,'" you read aloud.

The Cemetery Man?

Wasn't he the guy Ted asked about?

The one Coach Krump said didn't exist?

Then you hear a noise. *SCRAPE. SCRAPE. SCRAPE.*

The sound is coming from a grave. The one with the beaker on it. You aim your flashlight at the grave.

NO! This can't be real!

A hand is pushing its way up through the ground!

A moment later, a hideous head thrusts out into the air. The same thing is happening at the other graves.

The dead are rising!

Flee to PAGE 47.

About R.L. Stine

R.L. STINE is the most popular author in America. He is the creator of the *Goosebumps*, *Give Yourself Goosebumps*, *Fear Street*, and *Ghosts of Fear Street* series, among other popular books. He has written more than 100 scary novels for kids. Bob lives in New York City with his wife, Jane, teenage son, Matt, and dog, Nadine.

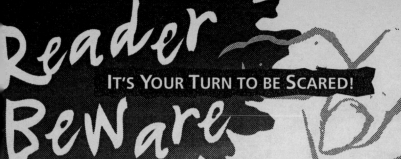

Reader Beware

Watch 1998 CREEP by with two great Goosebumps® calendars!

13 Stinky Scratch 'n Sniff Spots!

1998 CALENDAR

Goosebumps® 1998 Wall Calendar

Full-color covers of your favorite Goosebumps books as well as something new to scratch and sniff each month! Your wall will never be more horrifically decorated!

Goosebumps® 365 Scare-A-Day 1998 Calendar

Test your daily scare-how with cool Goosebumps trivia questions for every day of the year! Don't risk missing a day of spooky fun. (But don't peek ahead...you never know what will happen!)

Dare to be scared...every day of the year!
Calendars available at bookstores everywhere!